THE CRITICS ON CECILE PINEDA

Cecile Pineda is a writer of the utmost artistic integrity.
  – J. M. Coetzee

An author of powerful imagination and intellect, Cecile Pineda has already been compared to Cortazar, Borges, Marquez, Camus, Lagerquvist and Kafka. She has become one of the most discussed up-and-coming American novelists around.
  – San Antonio Light

Critical Praise for *Face:*

A poetic, hallucinatory work, finely and sparely written, the debut of a very talented writer indeed. May we see more?
  – Newsday

Written with sparse prose, stark drama and pointed symbolism, the novel is an intensely moving tale of catastrophe and redemption, of the fall and unyielding will of the human spirit. The prose of this novel cuts like a surgeon's scalpel; not a word is wasted or out of place.
  – Nashville Banner

There is an immediacy to her narrative, combined with images that startle our senses, that leave us haunted.
  – San Francisco Chronicle

Critical praise for *Frieze:*

Elegant form and vigorous detail give Frieze its mesmerizing power.
  – Josephine Humphreys in The Nation

A Singular, absorbing book.
  – The New Yorker

As delicately phrased as a prose poem. . . . A parable that opposes the pride and power of the state to the slow resistance of human life.
  – Richard Eder in The Los Angeles Times Book Review

Bardo99

Other novels by Cecile Pineda

Face

Frieze

The Love Queen of the Amazon

Fishlight:
A Dream of Childhood

Bardo99

a mononovel

Cecile Pineda

San Antonio, Texas
2002

Bardo99 © 2002
by Cecile Pineda

Cover illustration, "Angel Oscar"
© 1997 by Kathy Vargas

First Edition

ISBN: 0-930324-83-8 (paperback)

Wings Press
627 E. Guenther
San Antonio, Texas 78210
Phone/fax: (210) 271-7805

On-line catalogue and ordering:
www.wingspress.com

St. Philip's College (San Antonio, TX) Cataloging In Publication

Pineda, Cecile.
　　Bardo99 / Cecile Pineda.

　　　　　　110 p. ;　14 cm.
ISBN 0-930324-83-8 (pbk.)

1.Twentieth century—Fiction.　2. Viek, Joseph (Fictitious character)—Fiction.　3. Death—Fiction.　I. Title.

PS3566.I5214 B372 2002
813—dc21

for Maria Gilardin

*It was a place the local folk called Prypiat. When we
came there at first, many people told us that sometimes,
when it stormed, they could hear cries of battle in the
night. After the surveyors shot the grades for the new
city, we went in with the bulldozers. I was the foreman
of one crew. We began turning over the ground. Arms,
legs, hands, feet, skulls, the great rakes of the machines
turned them all up. One dismembered hand still
clutched the image of a woman. There must have been
thousands and thousands of skulls. We had uncovered a
World War II battleground. We couldn't dig enough
trenches to bury them all. We called the new city
Chernobyl after the exterminating angel. It was the
angel whose name is Wormwood.*

– from the account of Kyril Chernenko, 1918 - 2001

*O Nobly Born, thou hast come now to the time of the
closing of the womb-door. This is a time when earnest-
ness and pure love are necessary.*

– from the *Bardo Thodol*

I am alpha and omega.

– Revelations, xxii. 13

Bardo
99

bardo (bar´do), *n.*. [Tibetan, lit., *between two*.] The intermediate or astral state of the soul between death and rebirth.

Ringing, ringing, ringing, incessant ringing.

Where is he? Awakened from a plunging sleep, fumbling for the bell to silence it. The Angelus already. Must be. Clangor of an old story. Dreaming. Must have been. Rungs. Endless ladder rungs, hoisting himself up, tunneled in that wired cage, arm muscles screaming, leg muscles giving out. Endless spiralling rungs, straight to the roof. Ten? Ten storeys? Ten, or was it twenty? And all the while the sirens shrieking. Had his hands been free, he would have barred his ears.

All night the airwaves had been jammed, the regular frequencies commandeered in the emergency. He was on the point of giving up, tuning in the shortwave . . . someone must have come on the line.

– Joe Viek?
– Yes . . . ?
– Joseph Viek?
– Here.
– There's been an accident . . .
– an accident . . . ? *Dawn already!* He rubs his eyes.
– Afraid so. Yes.
– Where?
– Prypiat . . . not far from here . . .
 . . . and feels the shock, the turmoil in his chest . . . some pinwheeling comet, hurtling to earth, the thud of impact – oh God – Prypiat, the town he left behind when he married Myrna . . . and his brother, Otar, – dear God, it can't be – and all the others. . . . And the voice crackling through the speaker phone:
– Nothing to worry about. An evacuation has been ordered . . .
– What's the impact radius?

– We're not allowed to say.

Of course he's not surprised. They have to be careful, especially where people like himself are concerned.

– How soon can you be ready?

– Say again? (He can hardly hear: there's some commotion in the hallway, someone shouting . . .) Say again . . . ?

– Repeat: how soon can you be ready?

– Time to pack my bags, get my affairs in order . . .

– Your bags!?

(Someone shouting in the hall out there, he can't make out what they're saying . . .)

– My personal belongings – and my instruments . . .

– You don't seem to understand – you're over the weight limit as it is.

Weight limit. Perhaps they're being air dropped – what if the roads are blocked . . . ?

(He can hear them quite distinctly now: *Lift him higher. HIGHER.*)

– Maybe just a change of clothes.

No doubt they'll have all the necessary instruments and medical equipment on hand. Usual in these cases, after all. Set up emergency triage units, assign evacuation teams, appoint quarantine officers as the case requires . . .

HIGHER. LIFT HIM HIGHER.

– Say what? There's some commotion outside . . . I'm having trouble hearing you . . .

– . . . half an hour to be ready.

– Why don't I hail a cab . . . ?

– A cab! That's a good one: they've all been pressed into service. . . . The driver will be there for you in less than half an hour.

He remembers hearing the busy signal as the line goes dead and thinking it strange to be cut off so abruptly, making his habitual excuses: poor guy, must have his hands full in such an emergency – probably many more calls to make, how after all he himself is but a cog in the rescue machinery – many, many more among the conscripted with far more experience than he, and after all, now is not the time for self-indulgence.

Somehow he'll have to get the word to Myrna, there's no way to reach her at the plant, and Mammo – with the old age restrictions now in effect, her mother's no longer allowed a telephone.

He'll be gone for less than a week, no more certainly – grab a change of clothes, a toilet kit – and his daybook, a running record if questions ever come up – and they're inclined to come up more and more of late. A shame to leave his instruments behind. He feels empty handed without them, helpless almost, and now there's just time for a quick bite of something – a nice red apple perhaps – while he dashes off a note to Myrna. *Darling,* (mmmm, so tart against the tongue) *I've been called up. Nothing to worry about. Just another pesky accident –* he doesn't have to tell her where it is. *Don't wait up. I'll try calling you from out there if the lines aren't dead. If not, I'm thinking of you, my dearest,* and he scrawls his name, illegibly he thinks, and adds *Don't forget to look in on Mammo now and then!*

Here already. They've come for him. He can see the Land Rover down in the street flashing its hazard lights, splashing red through Myrna's lace curtains, on off, on off, reflecting against the apartment blocks across the street. Leave the note here, anchored by his half gnawed apple core – she'll be sure to see it when she clears the table – grab his bag, bolt down the endless corridor, past the closed apartments, their occupants inside, probably leaning against the doors, listening all of them, eyes glued to their peep holes.

– *Look out, for god's sake!*

In the far corridor, he makes out two figures in the stairwell, two men in top hats – undertakers, must be – silhouetted against the light, struggling to ease a stretcher

around the turn. Old Chowiek lying there – hands inert, trans-
parent on the coverlet. *Dead?* Is that what they're saying? Old
Chowiek? It can't be. Just yesterday, he tossed him the paper,
just yesterday: *Here, Viek: your daily lies,* and choked as
usual on his smoker's laugh. Just yesterday. He can't understand, but there's no time just now. They're waiting for him
downstairs. And these two, blocking the stairwell, about to
come to blows. . . .

    – *Shit! It's the last time. I've had it with these stiffs. I
keep telling you: it's the last time . . .*

    – Excuse me. If you'll let me by. I'm in something of a
hurry. And he squeezes his way past them in the narrow land-
ing, his back against the wall, takes the stairs two at a time
now.

    He can hear them, still at it up there, straining and
cursing, but already he sees the sunlight brightening the entry-
way; in another moment he'll be bursting through the panes,
out into the blinding glare.

    There they are, waiting for him, pulled up against the
curb, engine idling, exhaust steaming in the wintery air. Not a
moment too soon. The driver waits for him to vault aboard,
toss his bag into the overhead rack, and grab a seat before he
shuts the door. The van gives a lurch forward, and they're on
their way, five of them, not counting the driver. No one's talking. They're facing each other, bouncing about uncomfortably
as they skirt the frequent potholes, staring at nothing or dozing off, each immersed in his own thoughts, or peering out the
windows, trading glances now and then, exchanging pained
but forebearing smiles when the van happens over a particu-
larly nasty stretch. After all, it's an emergency. They all know
where they are headed, more or less, and training and experience have taught them what to expect. It's only a matter of
time before the driver reaches the first security barricade.

    He wishes they'd hurry – he has pressing work to do,
he's been assigned to the triage units – but the route winds the
usual slow way toward the river, across Exchange Place and

the Weaver's Green, past the Boulevard, and he marvels how
the city has changed in only 24 hours. Already the traffic has
been diverted, or commandeered. Nothing but emergency
vehicles on the road, Land Rovers mostly, identical to the one
he's riding. They roll past the government offices to where the
courts front on the Esplanade, the imposing facade recently
sandblasted to reveal its original golden color from before the
war. Now it glows in the slanting rays of the declining after-
noon. And on to the bridge, only the regularly spaced metal
grating to punctuate the steady hum of the tires and rushing
below, the roar of the Vlava, where it narrows . . .

And her – Myrna – that time. He sees her leaning over
the railing, her eyes fixed on the cascading water, having to
raise his own voice above the roar . . . *Myrna, please,* and sliding his arm around her waist, *you don't understand* . . . .and
when she turns her face to his, her eyes are wet with crying –
already a war widow at twenty, shy at having someone comfort
her.

He shakes his head, as if memory could be shaken free
like waterdrops.

Finally! They're leaving the city behind now for the
open country, part of what appears to be a long rescue cara-
van, traveling first in an easterly then southerly direction
toward Prypiat where he grew up as a boy. Toward the plant,
built with much press fanfare a few years back. With the slow
but regulated flow of emergency traffic, they'll reach the
impact zone roughly in another three hours or so. Mile after
mile, the countryside reveals itself, flat fields, still fallow for
the most part at this time of year, but here and there the soil
has already been disked in anticipation of the first planting; a
faint cast of green appears, cresting the furrows. The roadside
is overgrown with last year's stubble, turning to grey in the
spring rains. From where he sits, he can see a service road
running parallel to this one, choked with emergency vehicles
returning toward the city, flashing their blue code lights, signal of the civil defense teams.

A road security officer salutes them as the vehicle slows to a stop. They have reached the first emergency checkpoint. The officer wears paper boot coverings, a lead smock of the kind required by road security personnel. He reaches a gloved hand into the front window for the passenger manifest which the driver hands him affixed to a clipboard. He takes the list inside the guardhouse. They watch him through the shatterproof glass, talking with other personnel. At last he returns.

— Out, he commands. And take your personal effects. This vehicle is no longer in service.

Curious. He remembers stealing a furtive glance at one of his companion riders, but saying nothing. He reaches for his pack, tumbling it out of the rack, nearly hitting himself on his way out, down the steps, and out onto the roadbed. Shivering there in the cold, a slight wind blowing up from the east, from the direction of the danger zone. He wonders when they will be issued anticontamination masks.

— Documents, please.

He pulls off a glove, which he holds between his teeth, fumbling in his zippered pack to produce his rescue badge and civilian clearance. He waits his turn, casting an eye over the shoulder of his neighbor in time to see him produce an army discharge card as well, a card the man displays prominently. And thinks how he resents that bald kind of maneuvering. After all, in such an emergency there's little call for special treatment, but it comes as no surprise to hear the road security officer order him to fall out, and with a wave of his gloved hand, motion him toward the guardhouse area. Probably to be assigned to some cushy desk job where the air is pure.

— You, he says.

— Yes, sir!

— You're on the next bus. And he waves the driver away. They are left, teeth chattering, on the loading dock, watching the driver reverse the Land Rover and head back in the direction from which it came. Another vehicle pulls up, none too soon, presumably to take them the rest of the way. With the exclusion of the fifth man, only four are left headed for the target area. Back inside the vehicle, he turns to his neighbor.

– Does it seem unusual to you, this changing of vehicles?

– Not especially, no. They have to control the mileage range to limit the degree of known contamination.

– But wouldn't they issue us respirators?

– Maybe. Still a long way to go.

– Must be the breeder plant.

His neighbor shrugs.

– No one knows for sure.

And predictably, they are halted at the next checkpoint and made to leave their vehicle. As before, they are required to line up with their belongings while the road security officer checks their documents.

The first two in line produce some sort of laminated pass, much like a boarding pass. The officer examines these with unusual care. At last he directs them inside the guard house. When he emerges some time later, he wears a troubled look.

– Fall out! The officer motions him and his remaining companion. Report to the district officer on the double!

Not a good sign. Both of them are directed aboard a new vehicle, this one armed with metal plates. The banquettes are thinly upholstered in foam with a kind of fake leather covering – a holdover probably from the war. They take their seats opposite one another.

The road is unusually pitted, and the ride, though of relatively shorter distance, is the most uncomfortable – so far – of the day. The metal plates rattle alarmingly, evidently because the bolts have not been tightened in some time. A luminescent haze seems to be building up, thinning out the sunlight. He can see dense fog massing in the distance.

At the final checkpoint, they are ordered to remain in

the vehicle, waiting for the District Officer. The wait seems
interminable. The driver groans with impatience. He reaches
into his khaki jacket pocket for a pack of gum. They, all three
of them, sit staring straight ahead, wrapped in their private
thoughts. At last, a security officer comes on board to examine
their documents, his face masked behind the respirator
required of all frontline personnel.

– Out! He motions to his companion who sits more to
the front than he. He watches as the man reaches up for his
pack in the overhead rack. The man turns back briefly.

– So long, then. He waves.

He watches him leap down onto the roadbed. Outside
someone stops him briefly.

And now the officer stands before him, demanding his
identification, carefully scrutinizing his documents. His voice
sounds tinny through the respirator mouthpiece.

– When were you called?

– This morning.

– By your civilian rescue division?

He nods in reply.

– And who did you talk to?

He doesn't think he remembers. He's unsure. The officer re-examines his papers.

– No one appears to have signed your orders. And he
shows him the signature line. Blank. No avoiding it. White
space. Another delay.

– Wait here. The officer returns to the guardhouse,
perhaps to consult a supervisor, perhaps to confer directly
with the regional office, that is if the lines aren't down. He
waits. The driver chews gum, and the engine idles, discharging
plumes of exhaust into the frigid air.

At last, the road security officer towers over him once
more, scrawling something on a clipboard.

– Thought you were getting off easy, did you? He tears
a sheet off his clipboard.

– You're heading out. Report to the operations theater.

Back outside, he gives the Land Rover a smart rap. At once, the driver engages the clutch. With a sharp rattle of armor plates, the vehicle lurches forward once again.

At last! Once more he's on his way. He is aware of some release, a feeling of fatigue, perhaps. He allows himself to be lulled by the motor's hum, the rocking of the vehicle. He lets his thoughts precede him. Repeatedly he has been ordered to report to evacuation stations, field hospitals, really, or, when he did his foreign service, epidemic tents set up somewhere in the bush. This is the first time he's been assigned to a real hospital, probably a substantial installation, part of the new city, not the sort of temporary processing center he has been accustomed to – at least not until now. He can't help feeling pleased, although just how flattering is it really to be called in an emergency he knows so little about, even if it borders his home town?

In general, he knows what to expect: he knows the area. The fenced-in barracks just outside Prypiat, the dreary wood frame construction, and the peculiar clumsiness of the outdoor stairways leading to the second storeys, row after row, barracks reconverted from relocation sites following the war. Swinging his bag down from the overhead rack. Hopping down the corrugated steel steps. Saluted by the officer in charge. Signing the log. All familiar rituals. Reassuring. Nothing remarkable.

– *Long haul, eh?*
– *Not bad.*
– *Fog?*
– *Some. Yes.*

And the orderly stooping to take his bag.

– *Oh, and don't forget: mess at eighteen hours. Someone will show you to your quarters.*

Yessir. Competence. Everyone at his post. No hitch. No foul-ups. Gown and gloves ready and waiting at the donor station, nurse scrubbed and smiling under her neatly starched cap.

– *After all, it's a bit of an emergency.*

– Afraid so, Sir!

Correct. They're trained to be. Yes, the bureau has its
point. Satisfied. Removing the stethoscope from his ears.
Bending over the patient. Palpating. Two fingers: thump,
thump.

– Breathe. . . . Um, hmm. And how long has it been
like this? Um, hmm. Can't eat? Nothing stays down? Not even
water?

– Nosebleeds! Um, hmm. And when were you brought
in? Oh, yes, says so right here. Yes. Tongue? Um, hmm.
Coated. Open. Yes.

– Um, hmm. What's this swelling here? You've always
had it?

– No, no, nothing to worry about . . . When did you
notice it first..?

– Yes. The first time. Um, hmm.

Ah, well, yes. It comes to that, doesn't it? All of them,
bleeding, telltale petechiae. Vomiting. Diarrhea. Blind now.
Eyes burned out in the blast. Maybe run electrolytes. Blood
panel. Check his white cells . . . nothing much to do for him.

– Pain?

– Eh.

Order more morphine. Lots of useless nonsense in the
chart already. Always is . . . that time in Bhopal, or wherever
it was, *following explosion . . . um, hmm before evacuation*
patient inhaled . . . um, hmm . . . methyl isocyanate . . . um,
hmm.

– Lucky to get out alive . . . Not many . . .

– Lucky? Maybe not.

No. Sometimes better not to . . . and moving to the next
bed.

– How long has it been like this?

– Sir . . . ? Sir . . . ? the driver cuts into his reverie.

– We're here.

He stands up and stretches before reaching for his
bag.

– No, no, that's all right. Leave your gear. The orderly will pick it up.

– Oh?

– Leave it. They know you're here. They already phoned ahead.

Phoned ahead? When? Maybe from the district station. He doesn't bother to ask. He is tired, weary of the road, eager to get settled, get to work. He manages to swing open the door.

– So long, he waves as an afterthought.

He recognizes the plant from the news photographs. But a hospital? Here? The area must be an A zone. The building itself is of a curious design, round, with narrow vertical loophole windows, much like a blockhouse or an observatory. It is set at the back of a much larger installation. In the yard at the rear, an endless convoy of trucks passes in slow procession before disappearing out of view. To enter, he must pass through an airlock. An interesting feature. The entire building must be sealed off from contamination. Climate-controlled. The interior walls are cinder block, painted a dark grey, hung with the barest service lights. The lobby is silent, deserted. Unusual. Normally there should be someone on duty. He passes a number of doors, none marked, all locked. At the end of the passage, a sign reads ADMITTING. He reaches for the knob. It does not give. Strange. He knocks.

– Yes?

A small dark-complected little man holds the door slightly ajar, Indian probably.

– Can you tell me where to report?

– Report?

– Viek, Civilian Rescue Officer. You're expecting me, I think.

– Of course. Your orders, please.

He hands them over. The door closes once more. Now what? What if they notice something unusual? Curious, the fellow has not asked him in. At last he reappears.

– You're billeted on the third floor in the reception center. The orderly will bring your gear. Take the elevator to your left.

Formalities, more formalities. Patience, he tells himself. Patience. You've only just arrived. Still, he can't suppress the sense that he should be on the ward already, working with the triage officers. There's hardly any time to waste. And he must know any number of the victims . . . some of them his school mates, his childhood friends, probably . . . and his brother, Otar . . . And why do they insist on installing him on the third floor and in a windowless room to boot? What are they thinking of? Shutting him up – probably for the night. No knob. The door locks – but only from the outside as he shortly discovers. No phone, no way to communicate, or call for help. And what if there's an emergency during the night? what if there's a fire – or an explosion . . . ?

At least they've issued him pajamas. He tries the bottoms on. Exactly his size, and although he discovers the drawstring is missing and the top button as well, he manages to roll the waistband in on itself tightly enough to fasten it securely. He threads his arms one by one through the sleeves. He has trouble with the buttons. The holes are much too small to allow the buttons through. Yet when he manages at last to button them, he finds the holes are now enlarged. The jacket keeps flapping open. At last he gives up.

He lies down in the dark. Resting. Not thinking of anything. Feels the rocking. Hears the drone. The drone of some distant vehicle, a motor, idling perhaps. Succumbs to the murmur of the engine's hummmmm . . . .The driver up front, jaws working, quietly chewing gum. Something. Something happening outside where he can barely hear, a hurried whispering . . .

– Aw, ferchrissake, the driver fumes. He lets in the clutch. The car jerks forward.

– Wait! Wait! He grabs onto the driver's headrest, crouching next to him.

– If you don't mind, I'd like to know what's going on.

– Orders, goddamit, the driver hisses through clenched teeth.

– But that's the last barricade! We're inside the zone! We have no respirators. We haven't been issued iodine.

– Hold on! the driver shouts.

A sharp turn of the wheel sends him stumbling sideways. He grabs for his seat. He watches the driver's face in the rearview mirror, jaws grinding furiously. That's it. No explanation, complete disregard of orders. He's troubled by this, very troubled. The driver swings the vehicle onto an unpaved road. Where are they headed? Loose rock and gravel mark the way. From time to time a stone flies up and smacks against the windshield. The metal plates rattle and vibrate as if they are on the point of falling off. But the driver continues without reducing his speed, all the while cursing and muttering under his breath.

Nothing for it he thinks but to sit back and resign himself, clamp his hands tight to the banquette when the road gets nasty. Outside the ground lies flat and uncultivated. There are no trees, no distinguishing features other than the flatness and the ribbon of gravel which, given its siting, ought to project itself for miles with no curves or kinks at all, but – and he thinks this is very curious – it does nothing of the kind. It winds, it loops, it doubles back on itself occasionally, and here and there, abrupt hairpins cause him to grip the overhead rack to avoid being hurled sideways. At these moments, the driver apparently has all he can do to keep the vehicle on the road.

There is no sign of any habitation or facility of any kind. The fog settles lower and begins to obscure the meanderings of the road ahead, but the driver does nothing to slow his pace. A mild drizzle begins to pattern the windshield, moisture slowly accumulates, and before long, rivulets form. The driver seems to pay no heed.

Again he leaves his seat to crouch beside the wheel, grabbing onto the driver's headrest.

– Hadn't you better activate the windshield wipers?

– Windshield wipers! That's a good one: they haven't worked since Spring of '38!

The tires screech around the next curve which only just now comes into view.

– Goddammittohell, the driver screams, andtakeeverything with it!

Almost immediately another curve apparently catches the driver unprepared. The rear wheels seem to float in deep water. The vehicle begins plunging out of control, pitching over, the engine still running, rolling over and over, hurtling down a steep embankment, too fast for him to remember much: being thrown against something padded which catches him full in the face; tasting something hot and salty on his tongue.

He tries to stabilize himself on an overhead rack, holding to it fast with all his might but the vehicle keeps to its own appalling trajectory, tearing through undergrowth, smashing against stones and rocks, before it comes jolting to a halt. When he opens his eyes, he discovers his pack resting on the ceiling. He attempts to move. He touches his face. His hand comes away bloody. He thinks he may have cut himself against something. There is no sign of the driver. He drags himself forward on hands and knees, leaving blood prints in his wake. He feels a draft, a gust of wind. He looks to see where the cold air may be coming from: the door has been ripped from its hinges. He lets himself half jump, half tumble to the ground. The vehicle seems to have come to rest between two enormous boulders. Behind him, he catches sight of skid and swath marks, but the very thick mist that surrounds him makes it difficult to see. The incline is steep, and as he clambers upward toward the road, he discovers it is studded with vast stones and rocks which seem to balance precariously, looking as if they might become dislodged at the slightest touch. High above he can vaguely make out a terrace coming into view. He wonders at it: the entire way, the road appeared to pass through flat country.

He hauls himself up hand over hand, grappling with rocks and the occasional root. Inch by inch, his progress is painful and agonizingly slow. Halfway there, when he has to pause for breath, he catches sight of the driver far below. He straightens up as best he can, maintaining a precarious balance. The driver sprawls in a curiously crumpled position, one leg twisted at an improbable angle – a broken marionette.

– Hey! Hey,hey,hey,hey, his voice comes back to him. They must be entirely surrounded by mountains, although none is visible through the fog.

– Are you all right? Right,right,right,right.

He waits for his echo to play itself out but the driver does not move. Reaching him down there will be very difficult, dragging him out singlehandedly almost impossible. He begins to inch his way toward him, crawling sideways on all fours, taking care not to disturb any loose rocks above. At last he gets within speaking range.

– Hey. He bends towards him closer. Are you all right?
The driver seems not to have moved.
– Hey, he shakes him, hey.

Then he notices that the driver's leg is not twisted after all: his shinbone has snapped mid-calf. The foot dangles at right angles, exposing the bone. The fall seems to have wedged him fast against the base of a boulder.

– Hey! He hesitates. He begins to struggle with all his strength to free him, but from his awkward vantage point, it is next to impossible to flip him over. He manages to rock him slowly, tugging repeatedly, reaching the point of balance before turning him over on his back. One look at the driver's face tells him any further effort is useless. The driver – whoever he was – is dead. His skull is crushed, his face obliterated. Suddenly he becomes aware of a ringing in his ears. Hot bile wells up. He works to suppress the urge to vomit.

Good God, who could have imagined this turn of events? Leaving home – he checks his watch: 4:26 – barely four or five hours ago, with his orders unsigned, orders he had not even bothered to check, that he carelessly assumed were filled out correctly when he passed them over to the checkpoint officer, the fellow with the respirator – everything seemed normal, as routine as the half eaten apple core he left for Myrna, abandoned on the table.

How can he have allowed this to happen to him? It was to have been a routine assignment, nothing out of the ordinary. Another accident. Report to his destination. Receive further instructions. There would be wards to set up. They would assign him to one or another of them. He would have examinations to conduct, iodine to dole out. He would take patient histories – if the victims were still conscious. There would be staff assistants, coffee breaks. Now this. No idea of his final destination. No notion of which direction to take. The driver dead. No map, no indication of any kind. Good God, now what?

The fog seems to be lifting. Judging from their rate of travel, he thinks they may have come 30, maybe 35 kilometers from the final checkpoint. Not far. The last lap, so to speak. He must be somewhere inside the impact zone. Must be. Oh, God. And to be stranded here with a dead man, so mortally wounded as to be unrecognizable, probably even to his kin. His kin . . . he must have something, photographs, papers. Some indication, some map showing a final destination, circled in red perhaps, in his vest pocket somewhere, or perhaps some kind of document. He raises the driver's lapel, trying not to look, trying not to see the mangled face, runs his fingers along the inside lining, palpating, feeling, for a pocket. There. Something stiff, folded up inside. Oh, Christ, a newsclip, just what he needs. He lets the wind unfold it.

Prypiat, April 26. The department of civil defense today ordered the use of registered populations assigned to cleaning up contamination sites . . .

He watches the wind take the paper kiting down the slope. Pats the driver's pocket once more. Nothing. Is it possible? No identification. He palpates under the driver's buttocks. Something there, a wallet most probably. He's aware of some uneasiness, as if someone were watching, watching him loot the dead man's pockets. He extracts the wallet with some difficulty. He peers inside. Bills. One of them depicts a disembodied eye propped up against a painter's easel. Foreign tender, all of them, judging by their color. Little use for them in any case. Not here, not now. He lets the wallet drop to the ground.

Now what? His choices are limited ones at best, without a driver, with an inoperable vehicle, and without any clear indication of his destination. The most reasonable thing would be to trek the long way back to the final checkpoint, leaving some sign on the road, somehow pointing out his direction (although the road appears to be seldom travelled). On the other hand, there's the matter of contamination. Right now he is probably already inside condemned territory, closed to trespassers. Cesium everywhere. Products of decay: strontium, technium, God knows what. And you can't see it or taste it, or even feel it – not until much much later, when it's too late. Better not breathe, try not to inhale too deeply. Every moment of hesitation exposes him to doses beyond acceptable limits – that happy euphemism, Myrna calls it – and if that's not enough, he runs the risk of being shot as a trespasser. Where had he heard it: scavengers, some of them children, braving the barbed wire, crawling over mountains of waste, searching for what they can sell: contaminated syringes, medical waste, anything that could be salvaged and repackaged. Shot, many of them . . . .

No time to spare. And no point cowering inside the wreck of a lead-plated vehicle, waiting to be spotted down the deepest reach of an improbable ravine. All the same, perhaps he might find papers in the glove compartment, instructions, possibly water, and his pack, and whatever equipment he can muster. There may even be a map.

He straightens up. Is it possible? Now the fog has dissipated somewhat, he can see it plainly: the vehicle seems to be teetering precariously at the edge of a cliff. And although he discerns no sounds of water, it comes to him that probably there is a river or a stream running somewhere in the canyon far below. He begins to edge his way back down the slope, crouching, sometimes crawling, avoiding the huge rocks, the ones which seem to him the most unstable. He is about to clamber back inside the body of the wreck when something, some unknown thing prompts him to test its precarious balance before entrusting his weight back inside it. He barely touches it, a brush of the palm at most against the undercarriage, but even without the slightest pressure, there is a detonating roar. The explosion sends him sprawling backwards, smashing his back against a rock. Even from a distance of some 20 meters, he feels the searing heat against his face. Flame erupts within the chassis, soon engulfing it completely.

He feels the urge to laugh uproariously, not just because he is alive, not just because he seems miraculously to be uninjured, but because this very sinister column of black smoke billowing skyward may now provide the necessary distress signal that could very well save his life, or at least help extricate him from his predicament.

Once more he gets to his feet. He brushes himself off. He detects some possible abrasions, but otherwise he appears to have emerged no worse off than before. He begins again to struggle up the slope, hand over hand. From time to time, when he is forced to stop for air, he turns to watch the vehicle burning down below. Regaining the road must take him nearly half an hour, a physical effort that leaves him breathless, sprawled out on the gravel.

He has a fairly clear view of the surrounding landscape now the fog seems to have lifted. In the absence of map or compass, trying somehow to skirt or bypass the danger zone seems to him impossibly foolhardy. He considers what to do. He might arrange a marker in some deliberate configuration, a pile of stones perhaps, to draw attention to the wreck, or an arrow pointing toward the direction of the final checkpoint.

Or some word, yes, describing exactly his destination. Arrange pebbles in the roadway to read *Joe Viek. April 26. Returned to the vital checkpoint.* Vital? Why had he spelled it vital when it is final he means? Or perhaps use the reverse side of his orders. Of no value anyway: unsigned. But a pen. Where would he find a pen? Probably incinerated by now, along with everything else. Leave it. Better leave it like that.

He sets out, walking briskly. Perhaps it is the shifting light, but more and more he gets the feeling that nothing bordering this road seems remotely familiar. He has been walking for some fifteen minutes or so when the road twists abruptly to his left. Their vehicle did not pass this way. Of that he is certain. He stops. He decides to turn back. Roughly at the 14 minute mark, he begins to pay more careful attention to the roadbed for any signs of skidmarks. He continues, 15 minutes, 16, now 17. There is nothing. No indication. He determines to retrace his steps once more. He walks back for three minutes or so, now back and forth, purposely narrowing the stretch, until eventually he settles on a 20-yard span of road. He studies the shoulder to either side. No trace of skid marks, no sign of any wreck. He must have miscalculated.

He squats by the roadside, considering. Quite suddenly, out of the corner of his eye, he catches sight of a column of smoke. It seems to be rising from beyond the curve in the road, but at this distance, and from this vantage point, there is no way for him to pinpoint its origin. He straightens up. From a few yards back down the road, he catches sight of the burning hulk in the distance. It rests precariously at the edge of the precipice, charred now, gutted beyond recognition. But what is altogether strange is that now he is observing it from what appears to be the opposite side of the canyon.

Once more he retraces his steps in the direction of the ravine. Shortly (some 11 or so minutes from his most recent point of origin) the road forks, a deviation he thinks he may have failed to notice when he passed this way before. He stops to consider. He can't remember having come this way. He

decides it's best to keep to the main road, if this miserable
unpaved track can be identified as such. From time to time,
looking backward, he can still see the plume of smoke rising
faintly, its density rapidly dissipating, its color paling to
insignificance as the fire burns itself out. He turns a sharp
bend. Then he loses sight of it entirely. There is a steep drop
where the road ends abruptly, cut off by the ravine. On the
other side, he can see the point where it picks up once again.
There must have been a bridge here once, now there is no sign,
no way to cross, only the abrupt falling off, steeper than a
twenty-storey building. At the bottom, far below (he can see it
plainly now) is the riverbed, but it is a river gone dry. To the
right, far into the gorge, he has an unimpeded view of the
precipice. He spots what was once the Land Rover. The fire
seems to have burned itself out at last, leaving a blackened
hulk of twisted metal. As he watches, it slowly begins to tilt
outward. It breeches the point of balance, gathers momentum,
and topples toward the canyon floor below.

He's standing in the dry riverbed, surrounded by
gravel. Bending. Bending over, examining the traces: a sharp
declivity, exactly mimicking the outlines of the van, buried
now, probably liquefied beneath the surface of a subterranean
stream . . . Time: the first thing he thinks of. When he examines his watch, it reads 4:26, exactly when, to the minute, he
determined the driver was dead. He has the sense all this has
happened before. He holds his watch up to his ear. At first, he
hears nothing. Evidently it has stopped. His gaze wanders
aimlessly as he listens. Colors begin to meander across his field
of vision, reds, vermilions, carmines. He sits in the middle of
the riverbed, overcome with exhaustion.

The fog has lifted, but the overcast is dense. There is
no sun. Impossible to tell from its position therefore what may
be the time. There is no reason to think at this point that the
clouds may turn to rain. Or not. And he is without hat, or sun-
shade for that matter. Without water. Without a map of any
kind to pinpoint where he is, or in which direction to proceed.

His wristwatch appears no longer to be working, and soon, at
least relatively speaking, soon it will be night.

He tries to visualize the terrain surrounding the new
city, and the village – his village – and to call the map of
Prypiat to mind. It is a local map he has seen a hundred times,
but now his mind is blank. Absently, he pats his pocket. Of
course! It's still folded where he put it. Only when he extracts
it, he remembers it is the newspaper clip he pocketed earlier
as he crouched by the driver's side. He glances at it briefly
before discarding it. He holds his watch up to his ear. Now he
can hear its ticking distinctly. When he checks, the hands read
4:19. He finds it puzzling. Can he have jolted it without real-
izing? or did it start again of its own accord?

Something prompts him to stand up. He begins to
walk. He imagines any one of these desert tracks may lead to
something or somewhere. It is just a matter of time. The Land
Rover will be reported late or missing. Sooner or later they
will have to send out helicopters, rescue parties. It might help
if he had a flare, or some matches to light a fire at the very
least. But of course he gave up smoking – at Myrna's insistence
– five years ago.

What will she think when he is reported missing? On
an impulse, he looks back. The road, the very place where he
sat, where he was sitting but moments ago, is gone, or more
exactly, a fissure has inexplicably appeared, a slow yawning of
the ground, deepening rivers of air, the sort of thing that happens with erosion after months, or years, of waterflow.
Rivulets fan out, hardly noticeable at first, eventually deepening to gullies. Now, between the place where he crouched, and
the river gorge, there is a kind of camelback, a sharply rising
scarp. But there has been no disturbance, no earth movements
of any kind. Must be an active zone, he thinks, yet why had he
felt nothing, no tremors, no perceptible shocks? And had he
not turned around, he might have noticed nothing. That is the
most unsettling thing of all. He raises his watch to his ear. He
can distinguish its ticking very clearly now. It begins to occur

to him that, with the explosion, he may – temporarily at least
– have gone quite deaf, and he recalls that when the gutted
vehicle plunged to its final resting place, he heard nothing,
nothing at all.

He begins to walk as fast as possible. The track is barely wide enough here to allow two vehicles to pass. There is no
shoulder. The road consists of a bed of gravel, hard rock,
granite, possibly quartz, he decides, because of its faintly yellow cast. The landscape is flat. It stretches as far as the eye can
see. The road seems to run straight for some time through a
central valley contained to either side by a mountain range.
The valley itself is arid, without discernible vegetation. There
are no trees, certainly, not even sage or creosote. Thin wisps
of dried grasses blow in the wind, but only here, close to the
road. The soils show discernible signs of sedimentation laid
down in a bowl configuration. Once perhaps there was the
promise of water here when this may have been an inland lake,
but now there is nothing, no shadows, even the sun is absent.

He walks briskly without slackening his pace. He
thinks of nothing. He avoids looking. There is nothing to look
at out there anyway. From time to time, he imagines there is a
man ahead of him, a man like himself, walking ahead, alone,
head bent to the wind, bundled in a khaki jacket (although his
is a navy parka). Walking ahead, in this landscape, on this
road. Over this gravel. Not thinking – like himself. Not talking
to anyone. Not talking to himself. Walking. Only walking.
Saying nothing, thinking nothing.

The wind is chill now. He stuffs his hands in his parka.
Even so, it is cold, sunless. There is something curiously still,
no discernible sound, no bird. Only the man walking ahead,
leaning into the wind, thinking nothing, saying nothing, hands
buried in the pockets of his anorak. The wind does not whistle. From time to time, when he passes through a stretch bor-
dered by dried grasses, he imagines he can hear them rustle.

The road drops gradually to the valley's lowest point,
only to rise once more. He maintains his pace up the shallow

incline. He checks his watch from time to time. In another half
hour, an hour at the outside, he should reach the pass. He
walks briskly, trying not to feel the cold, trying not to notice
the peculiar cast of the light. Trying not to think. That time,
lying there, warm and comfortable, coming on Myrna's hair-
pin under the pillow, touching her long dark hair, watching
her open her eyes. Or watching her that time, setting the table.
All the little flowers falling. Falling on the cloth. Berries, ripe,
bouncing like marbles. No explanation. Or Mammo, losing her
hair by the fistful. No apparent reason. Lying there, and the
telephone call. *Exceed the weight limit as it is.*

    – *Civil defense.*
    – *What name?*

And old Chowiek. Dead. Invitation to a funeral. No
avoiding it. Probably someone else, maybe the one with his
discharge card, why not? Or the other two with their coded
passes. Or the one walking ahead in his khaki parka, not
thinking, saying nothing. Walking, only walking, hands in his
pockets, face bent to the wind.

    – *Fall out!*
    – *Radius?* Distinctly heard it. Testing? Testing. Must
be a firing range.
    – *Not allowed to say . . . .*
    – *Emergency (not far from P).* Whole valley. Nothing
growing. Twilight, bowl-like sedimentation. Bowl of light.
Barely see it. Chain of mountains. Chain of lakes. Promise of
water once, dried now. *Phosphorescent.* Man walking ahead,
straight ahead, head bent to the wind, trying not to talk, trying not to think. Rough going, hands buried deep in the pockets. Khaki parka, the one Myrna . . . Reported missing . . .

    – *We're not allowed to say.*
    – *Myrnahahahahahahhhh.*
    – *Emergency (not far from P).*

No sign . . . . Empty. Rooms stripped. Abandoned.
Left behind . . . wearing his navy parka, the one Myrna . . .

    – *Myrnahahahahahahhh.*

— Are you there? there? there? there?

Echoes. Strange. He doesn't remember any mountains. The road, track more like, hard rock, gravel. Granite, perhaps, or quartz. Ghostly pale in color, ghostly pale in hue. Yellow, yellow to yellowish. Keep walking. Hands, fingers frozen. No feeling. Numb. No gloves. No hat. Keep walking. Could have taken the driver's cap. *Hypothermia.* Might have known. Didn't think. Lying there still. If you . . . *hey, hey, hey.* Shouting hey, hey,hey,hey. Echo then. Chain of mountains. *Hey, hey, hey.* One. Two. One. Two. Right. Left. They say if you keep going. Keep walking. Man up ahead. Still walking. Hands deep in his pockets. Walking. Leaning into the wind. Not thinking, not saying anything. Hitting the pass. And behind? No one. Empty. *Now you see it, now you don't* . . .

Something down there. Lights. Lights far below. See them pulsing in the distance. Power station, must be, or hospital maybe. Take the better part of the night to reach. Walk. One foot. One foot before the other. *Minus thirteen.* One foot: left, right. Keep walking. Not thinking. Think of nothing. *Wind chill factor* . . . .can't feel anymore. Keep going. Far. Still far. Hands in his pockets. One. Two. Wind chill factor . . . Rest. Rest just for a minute. Lie down. Lie down perhaps. Huddle, just for a minute. Just time enough to get warm. In the ditch, perhaps. Lie down. That's it. Don't sleep, too cold for sleep. Minus thirteen. Mustn't. Mustn't drift off . . .

— Sleep, why don't you? Just for a minute . . . Viek . . . ?

. . . maybe not sleep. lie down, get warm . . . just for a moment . . . drift off . . .

— . . . in a bed . . .

— if only . . . a warm bed . . . any kind of bed . . . a place where one could lay one's head.

— a hospital bed maybe or even a stretcher . . .

— An ordinary bed, a bed with bars, say, retractable, where one can raise and lower the head at will . . . and the room is dark, the shades are drawn.

— Any kind of room . . . ?

– Dark, light, it doesn't matter. . . . Just so one could sleep. . . .

His open eyes are staring at the ceiling, at the walls. In the windowless room where the light overhead is nearly blinding. Just when he feels about to faint from hunger, an attendant pushes something at him through the porthole. He sits up. A tray: potatoes. Eggs of some kind. And gray links of sausage. The smell, somehow, doesn't encourage eating, nor does the color . . . perhaps because the light is artificial.

He places a forkful on his tongue. His jaws work to cut through what feels very much like rubber. Hears a grinding . . . his jaw? His jaw, perhaps? Stops. stops chewing. Detects the slight grating of the lock. The door swings open. Two men enter, not so much enter as shuffle in – heavy lead foot coverings, insulation suits. High contamination respirators.

– Joe Viek?

He spits the half-chewed stuff onto the plate.

– You are Joe Viek?

– Yes . . .

– We're here to take you to the ward. See you have everything you need.

About time. He rids himself of plate and fork. He moves rapidly toward the door.

– Just a minute. Where's your gear?

– Gear? I have just what I'm wearing. I'm still waiting for the orderly to bring my bag up from last night.

– You weren't issued pajamas?

– Oh, pajamas! There! He points to where they lie rumpled on the bed.

– Then you have been issued gear.

– Only pajamas.

– Yes. Could you put them on?

He chuckles.

– I had a little trouble with the buttons . . .

– No. Could we trouble you to put them on now?

– To go to the ward? Well, yes, why not? he laughs easily.

They're a lot more comfortable, especially if I'm going to be garbed all day like a mummy. He nods in their direction, but they seem somehow to miss the joke, waiting silently while he removes his clothing. He is about to thread his arms through the sleeves.

    – Your undershirt.

    – Remove my singlet?

    – Jockeys, too.

    – I don't understand.

    But they stay silent, waiting. He makes to hang his trousers on the hook provided.

    – No. Drop them, one says. You're ready.

    Outside the door, he catches sight of the digital lock. He must have been too tired to notice it when they let him in last night. The corridors are interminable. Doors at regular intervals. Digital code locks. They pass through a double glass-enclosed walkway between buildings to reach the elevator bank. They wait in silence. From where they're standing he can see into the yard. Outside the weather is rainy, overcast. One of the buildings is partially collapsed. On the roof a crew in lead contamination aprons shovels debris into wheel barrows – civilian workers probably, or scheduled populations. In the far distance, robots lumber back and forth, pushing debris off a ledge. Most of it rains down onto the bed of a dump truck parked below. Behind it, rows of empty trucks await their turn, engines idling, spewing exhaust in the wintery air.

    The doors slide open.

    – After you.

    He precedes them in the cage. One of his companions presses ten. The door closes. They exchange looks.

    – By the way, this is Doctor Chernoff. And I am Doctor Lipsey.

    – Doctor Viek. He extends his hand. They do not take it.

    – You *were* expecting me.

    – Yes, yes, of course, says Chernoff. We are expecting you.

The conversation ends there. An uncomfortable silence mutes the remainder of the ride. The tenth floor corridor gives on an isolation ward. There must be some twenty or so bunks in rows to either side. Patients perch, some of them, on the edge of their beds. Some sit quietly at the far end of the room where they have grouped their bedside chairs. There is no talking. One man vomits repeatedly into a kidney basin.

– Have all the patients been examined?

– Of course, says Chernoff.

They move down the ward.

– I'm afraid this is where you've been assigned, says Lipsey.

– You have instruments here that I can use?

– Instruments . . . ? They look at him blankly.

– I was told not to bring my own.

Chernoff seems troubled.

– I see.

Lipsey clears his throat.

– What we have here is a ward where we assign only people who were either present at the time of the explosion, or exposed immediately afterwards. (He drops his voice.) All of them have received . . .

– . . . doses beyond acceptable limits, he offers, nodding emphatically to show he understands.

– Yes, yes. Exactly, Chernoff picks up. Unfortunately, their prognosis is not at all encouraging. Foreign experts – Dr. Fault among them – are of the same opinion . . . .

– Yes, I'm aware of Dr. Fault's assessment . . .

They have come to a stop beside an empty bed.

– You're probably wondering why they have assigned you here . . .

– My CR unit wants me to further my training the better to respond in such emergencies . . . .

– Yes, of course. That would normally be the case . . .

– Unfortunately, Lipsey clears his throat, unfortunately here, no one is – shall we say – immune. We (he indicates his colleague) have been assigned because until now we have received no exposure whatsoever as far as anyone can tell. We will be here only for 24 hours to minimize our own risk. We will be evacuated when another fresh CR team takes over. This evening, to be exact.

– and I'm prepared to assist in whatever way I can . . .

Chernoff clears his throat.

– I'm afraid you don't quite understand . . .

– Understand . . . ? He stares at Chernoff in silence.

– Well, says Lipsey, don't you want to know why they assigned you here?

– My orders . . .

– No.

– Your orders are unsigned.

He feels himself begin to tremble. He slumps down on the edge of the unrumpled bed.

– Evidently you have received a dose beyond acceptable limits.

– Wait! He jumps to his feet. There must be some mistake. Let me see my dossier. Careful records were kept. Every assignment. I have my dosi tag to prove it.

– Where *is* your tag?

– Downstairs. In the reception building.

– There is no reception building.

– The building where I slept last night.

– You mean the holding cell.

– Very well, the holding cell, if you prefer . . . .

For the briefest instant a look passes between them.

– I'll phone downstairs, says Chernoff.

He makes to follow.

– No, says Lipsey, blocking his path, regulations require you to stay here.

– But . . .

– No contaminee is allowed beyond the door.

– Then I demand to see the attending! I have work to do!

— Calm yourself, calm yourself, urges Lipsey. We are the attendings. There's no need to shout. You'll disturb the other patients. I'm sure all of this can be resolved in a reasonable manner.

The doors swing open. Chernoff strides back in.

— It's as I thought. They already canned it.

— *Canned it?*

— Don't shout. You'll disturb the other patients.

— I want an explanation.

— They always can everything when the patient is transferred, everything in the holding cell, explains Chernoff. Everything is sealed. To avoid contamination. Every stitch and scrap – all articles of clothing. Shoes. Toiletries. It's for your own safety, and the safety of the other patients.

Lipsey nods.

— They can everything. Even the bed.

— The bed?

— Yes, the bed you slept on.

— When a new contaminee arrives, a new bed is provided.

— Even the walls of the holding cells. They're programmed to be self-destructing. Every one. Digital codes.

— But my tag was in there!

— There's no need to make a fuss. In due time, we'll reach your unit chief, Brixton, isn't it? We'll track down your dossier.

— But you say you leave tonight.

— We leave tonight, yes. But there are others who'll replace us.

— But they'll leave tomorrow!

— Look, we have made every provision for your safety – at least while you're here. There are writing materials, things to read, you can even play chess – or solitaire, if you prefer. You'll stay here with the other patients. Your records will be found, no doubt, within a day or so, and if the combined totals read within normal limits, you'll be allowed to go.

– Meanwhile, this is your bunk, says Chernoff.

– Bed number twenty, sighs Lipsey, his tone suddenly going soft.

– Ward number 99. Chernoff notes something on his clipboard.

They make for the exit doors. He doesn't try to stop them. Why? And what is it about him, about the situation, that turns him into an abject shadow of who he really is? Is it the atmosphere? the rows of beds? Have they managed to convince him? Is he ready for the waste dump? Consigned to let his bones decalcify in this so-called hospital? And what about the disaster victims – the people from his village? And his brother? Don't they need all the help that they can get? An outrage! Someone will hear about this. Someone will know. When he gets out, he's going to make an awful stink, they can be sure of that! What happened to him may happen to others. And Myrna! Eventually Myrna will realize something is amiss, make no mistake! She'll notify the authorities, call the bureau, contact his unit chief. And Brixton! In all probability Brixton is already puzzling why he failed to show up.

– *Wait a minute, wait a minute, gentlemen! Everyone makes mistakes. Just a normal foul-up. After all, we've got to hold our own against the military!* Gales of laughter. A regular guy. One of the fellows. Oh, they like a game remark now and then, all right. It livens things up. Especially Brixton. Nothing like a little joke to break the tension. It's only a matter of time. But wait! His orders were unsigned. One after the other, all the others were dropped off. Was that why? Of course, of course. The bureau must have known from the beginning. He must have been exposed. They must have planned, knowing he would wind up here, unable to leave, in a hermetically sealed ward where the air can neither leave nor enter.

He scans the room. He recognizes no one. But it's a state of emergency, all right: everyone here has lost his hair, or almost all of it. Although not everyone displays the usual advanced symptoms: skin lesions, nausea, bleeding from the nose. Some seem virtually symptom-free. They eat, some of them, with much more gusto than he can muster. He suspects he is upset. When the lunch tray arrives, he barely picks at his food. He exchanges plates with his neighbor when the orderly is not watching, his full for his neighbor's empty. Better not give them the wrong idea. Some of the patients are even women! He can identify them by their voices – high, freakish. Like children. There's even a woman in the next bed, lying close to the wall. Sometimes her eyes open but do not focus. He's not sure if she can see him.

He wishes there were something to do to keep his mind occupied. Some patients read. There are magazines here and there, scattered on the bedside tables. Fashions. Racing cars. Electronics. There is even an issue given entirely to hunting and fishing. He chooses to play a game of cards with someone in number 2 bed, someone with his own deck – probably smuggled in, concealed under his official clothing, four suits, but there the resemblance ends. Animals. Fish. Birds. Snakes. He's never seen anything quite like it. Clubs are fish, his partner keeps reminding him. Hearts are birds if you just remember. But it is utterly confusing, trying to keep track of which is which. At last, he gives up altogether.

– I'm sorry, I have no mind for it just now.

– But you passed through the corridor, didn't you? When you came here? The passageway that connects this building with the receiving center? When they brought you in?

– Nobody *brought* me here. I came because I . . . .He discovers he is shouting. His hands are trembling. He drops his voice to a whisper. Look, just leave me alone. I'm not here to answer questions. I'm just waiting for my discharge.

– You don't think they'll let you go now, do you? After what you've seen?

– What are you talking about? There's nothing here any different from anywhere else, is there?

– You can see very plainly what they're up to out

there. He casts a furtive eye toward the demolition yard.

– You mean the decontamination crew? That's just normal procedure whenever there's an accident. All I know is I'm stuck in here. They won't let me out. They can't even seem to find my dossier.

– Your dossier? Is that what they told you? Your dossier is part of your chart, and there'd be no reason to admit you if they didn't have your chart! It's probably out there right now. By the nursing station. Just ask them. They'll show you anything you like.

– What are you telling me? You mean I only have to ask?

– Of course, just ask the attending.

– Chernoff? Or Lipsey?

He shrugs.

– Chernoff. Lipsey. Yesterday, today, tomorrow, it doesn't really matter who it is. They all use the same name anyway. It just makes it easier to remember for the patients with amnesia. Just ask for Chernoff. Or Lipsey, if you prefer. Carrot or stick, it comes to the same thing.

There's no point arguing. It's the oiliness of the fellow's smile, a greasy kind of condescension that seems to insinuate he, Viek, is diseased like all the other patients. As if he didn't know the score, completely out of it, like the woman in the next bed, for instance, who does nothing but sleep. Except that sometimes her eyes are open. But he is fairly certain she sees nothing. He thinks she must be comatose, although he knows she responds to sound. He looks for her chart, but the rack at the bottom of her bed is empty. At least this one seems not to have been exposed, or why would she still keep a full head of hair? Thank God his own hair loss has been very minimal as well – at least so far. A few strands here and there. Quite normal, really, and there's no point drawing anyone's attention to it . . . if he combs himself lightly . . . and at night, when no one is watching, drops his combings in with his neighbor's waste . . . . The woman's eyes are shut tight, most of the

time anyway. . . . Although just now her eyelids flickered. He
stands by, as quietly as possible, watching her. She opens her
eyes. She is not dead, not nearly! Although no one would ever
know it from the kind of care they give her. No one comes to
feed her, nor is there any effort to clean her or even change
her bed.

    – Does it hurt? he whispers. Do you have pain?

    No response.

    – Blink! One for yes, two for no. Any pain?

    She doesn't blink. Her eyelids do not flutter. She does
a curious thing. She smiles. It is only the ghost of a smile, the
faintest lifting at the corners of the mouth, but he is certain he
is not mistaken. She is quite beautiful still. If he had his stethoscope, he could listen to her heart. If they kept the charts at
the bedside, he could learn her name. If they keep any charts
at all, it's behind closed doors, locked outside, in the nursing
station. Except sometimes the doors swing open for the
briefest instant, when a nurse comes through. Perhaps if his
bed were situated closer to the door, he might be able to see
better.

    – Would you like to have a look outside?

    He can barely make out who is speaking to him. In the
yard outside, high intensity carbon arc lights are mounted
everywhere for the emergency crews to continue working
through the night. In their reflection, he can see that, unlike
the other patients, at least his interlocutor still has hair, long
matted strands of it.

    – But I thought they didn't allow anyone out there.

    His interlocutor laughs softly.

    – Sure. That's what they have to tell you because that's
what everyone believes. What do you think they're doing out
there? He points toward the swinging doors.

    – At the nursing station?

    – Not so loud!

    – Look, I don't know what you're getting at. . . .

    – Didn't you pass through the corridor . . . ?

– What corridor?

– When they brought you here.

– Nobody *brought* me here, I *volunteered* to come
here. I'm a civilian rescue officer. Prypiat is my village! And
now I'm stuck! They won't let me out! He tries to compose
himself, to lower his voice. They say they're waiting for my
dossier.

– Your dossier? But they keep all of them out there!
They have everyone's dossier. At the nursing station. It's part
of your chart. They can't admit you without a dossier.

– How do you know?

– Because my bed is situated near the door. Sometimes, when a nurse comes through you can catch a glimpse of
them out there. If you like, I could rent you time . . .

– I don't understand.

– I could rent you time in my bed. On the night shift.
That's when it's best to see, like now, when it's dark in here,
but light out there.

– I don't think so. Anyway, I don't have any money
right now to pay you with . . . .

– Burned it, did they? Is that what they told you? He
laughs, not so much a laugh as a cackle. Never mind.
Everyone here owes me royalties.

– How's that?

– Everyone wants to know what goes on out there and
I'm the only one who can let them see it. But they have to
reserve with me several nights ahead. They take their chance,
of course. There are no guarantees. They might occupy for an
entire night and the doors might not swing open once. And if
someone does come through, it swings open very fast. You have
to pay careful attention. There are only two back and forths
worth anything. After that, you have only increasingly minor
oscillations until the doors come to rest. Sometimes an occu-
pant will fall asleep, unable to stay awake long enough to see
and will miss it altogether. Then of course they go on the wait
list for another night. Or sometimes they reserve only a part of

a night. But of course there are no assurances the doors will open at any given time. Sometimes a client occupies and just after his shift is over and I return him to his bed, the doors will open. I have everything I can do to get under the covers myself in time for them not to see me.

    – You mean to say out there they know nothing of your rental scheme?

    – Of course not. If they caught on they would make me change my bed. Don't you want to sample it for a while? He raises the sheet – a clear invitation for him to slip in.

    The bed appears rumpled, the sheets stale. But his interlocutor turns insistent.

    – Go ahead! Climb in. Lie on your side – your head propped on your arm – that's right. That way you can see better – and the position is uncomfortable enough, you won't be lulled to sleep. I'll come get you after your viewing time is up.

    He can't imagine why the bed feels so cold and damp. Perhaps it's because the blankets are too short, and here and there it's obvious the weave is wearing thin. He pulls the covers about himself as tightly as he can. Combs keep turning up between the sheets, under the pillow, even tucked inside the pillow case.

    – Try to leave the bed exactly as you found it. It makes it more comfortable for the next occupant. It's so unpleasant to find a strand of someone else's hair, don't you think, just when you're becoming so used to it, it almost seems like your own bed – without having to be reminded. I know I feel very sensitive about it myself.

    – Then what are all these combs doing in here?

    – Combs? Oh, those! People pay me in combs sometimes – when they no longer have any use for them They're part of my collection. Some are genuine tortoise shell! One patient even paid me with a silver comb and brush set, imagine. I let her have a week.

    – A week in your bed?

    – Well, only at night. I only let her in at night.

– Did she find out? About her dossier?

– Hmmmm. I'm trying to remember. That was when I
first came here. Well of course, things were different then. For
one thing, they kept the linen cleaner, and there were more
blankets to go around. I think she fell asleep. Yes, if I'm not
mistaken. She got tired of waiting. Yes, that was the one. When
I came to tell her her time was up, I found – it pains me even
to think of it – I found she was cold! Imagine! No one knows
how long she had been lying there like that. And I had to get
her back to her own bed in time so no one would notice! I kept
the comb and I inherited the brush as well. She would have
wanted it that way. After all, the staff would only help themselves. It's a wonder she had anything left, poor dear, with all
the stealing that goes on.

– *Stealing?*

– Oh, yes! You can't imagine! You can't leave anything
out, not for a moment. I wear everything I have. If you don't,
it disappears. People have even had their dentures taken! You
can't even take them out at night!

– What would anyone want with someone else's dentures?

– They sell them.

– *Sell them?*

– For the gold. Dentures, suitcases, even hair. You can
see whole museum cases full of things downstairs!

– Are you saying you're free to come and go?

– Of course! I'm the night watchman! They give me
room and board. I'm allowed to sleep in here during the day.
They even let me in the museum.

– By day?

– Well, no. Not exactly. That wouldn't be fair to the
paying crowd. They only let me in at night. Anyway, it's not
exactly a museum. Would you like to take a look? I can let you
down there if you keep it confidential . . .

– But won't they notice me? In there?

– At night? Oh, no! No one pays any attention. If anyone sees you, they'll just think you're one of the custodians. They let them through all the time. Just remember to keep your eyes down, as much as possible. Always focus on the floor. That way, they'll think you're looking for the dust.

It comes so easily, this means of escape! Why not? He'll find a way to make a run for it . . . when no one's looking, when his guide is momentarily distracted. . . .

In the dark stairwell he follows the tread of his guide's footsteps, feeling his way along the wall. Already the mere sound of his palm rubbing against the plaster strikes him as reassuring.

– Just a little further down here there's a switch I know about. They always keep it dark in here at night. Saving power probably. I can never find the main switch, but at least you'll see the exhibits.

He flicks on the lights.

– This place used to be called the Yugoslav Hotel but now they use it like a store room.

An endless succession of dioramas lines the walls, museum cases, each lit with its own light, although the hall itself remains in darkness. There are cases with nothing but eyeglasses. Cases of dental appliances and false teeth. One even contains a mound of ancient shoes.

– I don't understand. What happened to the exhibits? Why is this in a display case? It's just a pile of shoes.

– No, that *is* the exhibit. It's hermetically sealed in glass for the comfort of the spectators. Can you imagine inhaling all that human odor? Mind you, I'm not the curator here, but quite confidentially, I understand they're unusual for dioramas. Normally they use plaster of Paris to create verisimilitude. But here, everything real you see is here.

– Yes, but nothing much is happening.

– Happening? You want something to happen?

– The shoes, for instance. Now if someone were wearing them some place, a street scene or something . . .

– You don't have to wear shoes for them to be real.

Look at these eyeglasses. You don't have to wear eyeglasses all
the time, but they're still real . . . .

He stands examining the eyeglass diorama, a termite's
ziggurat of gold and wire and tortoise shell.

– But they're not even eyeglasses. They're just frames,
none of them have lenses . . . What happened to the glass? and
here . . . what's this? this mound of wool?

– In the next exhibit? That's not wool! That's hair,
human hair. For weaving into blankets . . .

– Blankets?

– For the bunks. Upstairs. To keep the inmates warm.
Everything sterilized. Processed in the most sanitary condi-
tions. You'll see. I'll take you through the work rooms . . .

– If you don't mind, I think I've seen enough.

They are at the far end of the room, their path blocked
by a makeshift barrier. A deitz lamp flashes on and off.

– Don't mind this. You can still get in. Normally this
section would be closed off. It's not part of the regular
exhibits. They've been storing things in here till they have time
to sort them out. Merchandize keeps coming in . . .

– Merchandize . . . ?

– Well, in a manner of speaking. It's really not for sale
– although of course they charge admission – and they tell me
the depots are already full to overflowing. There's a huge
back-up, some say at least fifty years worth, maybe even
more! The curators haven't had time to get around to it with
all the new material coming in all the time. That's why the collection is so haphazard: the candlesticks, the ritual objects . . .

– and these baby clothes . . .

– Well, of course, I didn't want to say anything. It's a
little – sticky, shall we say? In fact they're not sure they should
archive any of this just yet. Trial visitors have trouble when
they see this part . . . .Confidentially, that's why it's temporarily roped off. They can't tell if it's the ritual objects, the
prayer shawls . . .

– prayer shawls . . .

– Yes. But maybe it's the baby clothes. People like to get sentimental when it comes to children, don't they . . . ? But of course they don't realize: these are just the clothes . . .

– Perhaps we could leave now? Isn't there another exit?

– Wait! Every time I take someone through here I have to put out all the lights. Safety precaution. Especially at night. They're not on automatic timers.

He scans the room for a possible escape, but the room becomes dark suddenly, lit only by the warning pulse of the deitz lamp. He feels his way in the dark of the corridor. The guide's voice drones on in the semi-darkness.

– Here. This way. There's just one more thing I have to show you.

He follows the sound of the guide's voice. He wonders where they are, where the guide may be taking him. This is not the way they came.

A few more steps and the wall gives way. The guide switches on a light and fumbles with a loaded key ring in the sudden brightness. They have come to a door recessed in the wall of the corridor, a janitor's closet – another diorama probably, this one of mops and brooms and buckets. He badly wants to run, but the guide blocks the entrance. He reaches for an overhead cord. Inside the narrow confines of the closet a naked light bulb swings back and forth, back and forth, etching now one wall, now another in sharp relief. Row upon row of old manikins, tubby, middle aged men in rumpled suits and grey fedoras, some of them still holding long-extinguished cigars between thumb and forefinger as if in their bemusement they had let the fiery coal go out, their broken wings affixed to their decaying backs, repaired long ago with pressure tape or dried out dribbles of epoxy, stored haphazardly, piled on one another, frozen in sitting positions, perched now on thin air, others leaning sideways, about to topple over. He detects hardly any smell, the mustiness of enclosed places perhaps, the staleness of once-worn clothes . . . .He can't suppress a sigh. The guide laughs silently.

– Our collection of exterminating angels. You expected
radiance perhaps? Go ahead: it's safe to touch them. They're
disconnected now. You won't get a shock.

He stretches a hand out with some reluctance: the
dust, the mustiness repel him. Accidentally he knocks against
one of them, but the figure merely yaws sideways, rocking
imperceptibly, its damaged wings briefly fluttering, releasing
particles of dust. The guide suppresses a wracking cough.

– Styrofoam, he chokes, all carved out of styrofoam.
Lightweight material – so they could fly. The complete collection. Well, almost. One is missing. No one's found it yet. They
searched all along the cornices, the roof, the entire pediment.
No luck. Because of course they have to decommission it
before it's too late.

– Too late for what?

But the guide doesn't answer. He extinguishes the
light. They return to the hallway. He locks the door behind
him. A sign warns 'high voltage'. The 'danger' has been
scratched out.

The guide eyes him non-commitally, the expression on
his face impassive.

– Yes, indeed, he says. They were powerful. Once. All
except the missing one.

– How do they know they haven't found them all?

– You mean the missing one? He drops his voice
although there is no one to overhear. Because the oscillators
still show delivery of more than a million volts. The current
isn't dead. Which is why no one manages to escape from here.
You weren't planning to try it, of course, but just in case, it's
a kindness to warn anyone. One of my clients tried it once . . .
hurled himself against the fence . . .

– Can we leave now?

– Sorry. I can see how anxious you are to go, but the
doors in this wing have to be self-locking – traffic control, you
understand – but on your way out, we'll pass by the suitcase

exhibit, and you'll be able to get a glimpse. It's our most popular one, the one tourists come from everywhere to see.

– I don't care about any suitcases. Just get me out of here . . .

– Relax, man. There's plenty of time. No use getting all wound up. All the lights here are on timers, we only have a minute anyway . . .

He stands examining the suitcase collection; he notes the names printed on them, the addresses written in large, the hurried scrawls, certain identification, protection against loss. They must have belonged to someone . . . someone must have tied a rope around them once when the contents became too much to carry . . . .

– Here, look at this: Aboulafia – there's your "A;" Abrabanel; Ben Jouloun; Castelnuovo – a concordance, really – and the streets: all alphabetical: rue du Roi de Sicile, rue du Rosier . . . .By name, by street, by city, by country, all alphabetical . . . I don't know if you realize the considerable effort it took to get all the transit names and the former addresses to conform. He hears the guide's voice droning on, growing louder, louder: Dreifuss, Esformes, Faganboym, Galperin, Haskovec, Isaakson, Jacobo, Kaplanoff, Lekhtman, Levinsohn, Mourad, Naftaly, Nathanson, Otolenghi, Peretz, Polakoff, Portuges, Quattelbaum, Quittner, Roatcap, Rosen, Rosenbaum, Rosenblatt, Rosenbleuth, Rosenbloom, Rosenfeld, Rosenkopf, Rosensteyn, Rosenthal, Rosenwald, Rosenzweig, . . .

The names, the names. There is no end. *Alphabet of the damned!*

He's tumbling, tumbling, his body turning inside out, floating through the chambers of some turreted cell, all light, all made of color – luminous, yes: *Abouoolafiaaaaahhhhh* . Crawling through its echo, *Abouoolafiaaaahh,* . . . He bends his worm's body around the corners of "A," spirals through "B," churns around "C," crawls through the names of cities and towns and streets, Street of the King of Sicily and Street

of the Rose Arbor, and the trellises and graveled walkways,
and the topiary all neatly clipped, black iron crosses sprout-
ing alien members. The voices are too raucous, the clapping
too loud, the music too martial, the colors too red, too
swirling, rest, if only he could rest . . . He's tired, he wants to
sit down,

     – that's right, sit down, why don't you . . . ? Viek?

     and his eyes throb, pulsing rainbow colors: the wash of
dawn, sunset blush, green bite of twilight sky, jagged halos,
shimmering, oscillating like water,

     – blink, blink, Viek . . . once, twice . . . .All you have
to do is blink.

     a sharp wave in his skull but no sound, the light, it
must have been, the sudden jolt from dark to light, if he just
sits still, sits still here for a moment, shuts his eyes . . .

     – Shut your eyes.

     he wants to close his eyes, blot out the pulse, the throb-
bing in his head,

     – Smell the roses . . .

     he's feeling dry, empty. water, water, that's all he
needs. he wants to sit here and never get up. . . .

     – Breathe, Viek, remember to breathe.

     what happened to him? an accident? was it? something
he can't even remember? can't remember any more . . .

     – What are you doing?

     . . . sitting.

     – Sitting and . . . ?

     . . . sitting and shutting my eyes. closing them to light.

     – When there's still so much to see?

     . . . done seeing. done seeing for a time.

     – Open them.

     Shut tight . . .

     – Open them. Now.

     Red . . . .Roses, all of them. Red, too red, swirling with
an brilliance such as he has never before seen. Millions of
them. And alleys. Gravel walkways: a maze edged in boxwood,

a rose garden – is it? – Yes.

    – Try standing up. Bend forward. Bear down with your . . . .That's it. A little more. Now rise. Rise . . . that's it! Stand up! How does it feel?

    . . . shaky . . .

    – Shaky and . . . ?

    . . . i don't know . . .

    – Try a few steps. Come on . . . right . . . .Now left . . .

    . . . wobbly . . . need to lie down . . . .

    – Lie down?! Come on, Viek – it's not yet time, goddamn it . . . one step . . . now another . . . .Not finished yet, are you? Are you? Viek? Viek?

    – Not finished yet, no, not yet, goddammit. (Think of something stupid like that, you get a rose garden, for godsake. Banal. A trashy musical . . . .)

    – Dreamed it all up, didn't you?

    . . . roses! each one, each bush, ringed with a clever little moat, irrigation basin, all nicely laid out, staked, each with its own designation, all in order, nothing left to chance . . .

    But no. When he looks, when he looks carefully, he sees their leaves have begun curling, wilting at the edges, and here and there, the great crimson blossoms seem to droop with their own weight. Oh yes, he can just see himself irrigating, edging his way between the thorns, tilting a watering can, waiting for the pit dug around each crown to fill to overflowing, row on row, as far as the eye can see, big enough to be the rooftop of the world, must be, and where would he get water . . . ? A clown act, this one: He's tired? a bench appears. Smell the roses? a garden appears. Water? now a spigot appears. Enough to make you cry. If he places the can beneath the spigot, if he turns the tap, if he waits for the can to fill . . . .Enough of such absurdities. He has no time for this. He should be with his triage unit.

    – Delaying?

    Of course, of course he knows he is delaying. If he begins with the fartherest row, he will have to carry water as far as the eye can see . . . And there's no time, no time left.

     – Viek? Why not start with the nearest row: enjoy the satisfaction of immediate results . . .

     Why is he doing this? He turns the spigot off. Lift from the center. That's it. Weightless. Light as a feather is light. He could fly!

     – Eh, Viek . . .

     Well, maybe not a feather, heavier than a feather . . .

     – Viek? Easy with the can.

     And stones in the pathway, sharp enough to make you trip . . .

     – Stones?

     – All right, a stone, a small stone. Not a big stone, not a rock. Not a very big rock, a small stone, smallish . . .

     – Viek?

     A pebble possibly, round. Shiny. A black pebble . . .

     – Faster.

     – All right. If you're going to nag, I quit.

     – But you've only just begun. You can't quit: what if they die?

     – The roses? They're garish anyway. So what if they die: I'll be free to go!

     – Back to the museum . . . ?

     – Been through the museum . . .

     – There's always occasion for a little return visit . . .

     How has he come to this predicament? Imagined it, perhaps . . .

     – Stop! Viek! Watch out!

     Watch his step. Avoid the ruts where the path gives way. Where he'll stumble on the unexpected stone. The sole of his shoe has come separated from the upper, come unglued: too much water, too much wet, perhaps, that time, Myrna . . . must be on his guard, watchful, especially watchful not to trip, to spill, cautious not to spill the precious drops . . .

     – Viek?

     – *What?* Remember not to trip, not to . . .

– Watch your step . . . You're nearly half way there.

The going rough, nearer now by half. Nearly half already. The last row far as the eye can see, nearer . . .

– Watch out!

. . . always like that, the least little scare, hot, hot under the collar, sweat breaking out, the nape hairs wringing wet, the least little hesitation, loss of footing, watch your step, skirt the rough places . . . the . . .

– Viek?

– *What now?*

– No need to be impatient . . .

. . . didn't ask for this . . . stones studding the path . . . protruding. Great round stones, river stones, catch you unawares . . .

– Signs of self pity? An unattractive trait. What's so special about you, anyway?

– *Go to hell, why don't you?*

– That's it, Viek. A little spunk, a little feist. You can do it!

– *Get fucked, forgodsake!*

– Now you've done it. Nearly tripped, nearly gone sprawling. Wasted precious water needlessly. Lucky fellow. It could have gone badly. It could have been your blood! Nearly there. One more row . . . one more now, and then you're free! Viek? Viek, are you there?

– yes, i'm here.

– The last row? Viek?

– the last row in this section . . .

– What's it say?

He bends to read the identifying tag. Words once written there. The legend erased now. Corroded. Marks now. Indecipherable

– Barely make it out. *Ma . . . . Madame.* Looks like Madame . . .

– Madame what?

– Madame . . .

– All roses are named Madame. Madame *what?*
– Madame . . . *Mo* . . . *Moz* . . . Wiped out . . . *Mozote!*
– Yes. Mozote.

But they're all wiped out . . . can't make the names out anymore. . . . Roatcap, Rosen, Rosenbaum, Rosenblatt, Rosenbleuth, Rosenbloom, Rosenfeld, Rosenkopf, Rosensteyn, Rosenthal, Rosenwald, Rosenzweig, all wiped out . . .

The ground is hard, caked, but black somehow, oxidized. And the smell . . . once familiar . . . . Rot? rot . . . dead meat. That's it. Otar. Otar who used to feed his roses blood discarded from the lab . . . . Clear out the path, dig out the stones. Brace his right foot against the shovel's blade, incline his weight. Lean with all his might. Something hard, something grating against his blade. And now it comes more clearly into view: rounded, smoothed by water, a river stone, there it is, emerging from beneath the surface. He stops to rest, to wipe his brow and in the far distance, he catches sight of other men, as far as the eye can see, spread apart, mirrored in a waterless lake . . . digging, submerged to their thighs, wading in their own reflections. Too far distant to call out . . . .Digging. He watches them brace a foot against the blade, bend their weight, pull shovelfuls of sludge, piling up the mud, digging, pulling up river stones, mounds of stones, rounded, smoothed by river water.

– Viek?

Once more. Once more he thrusts his weight against the blade, rocking the shovel, now forward, now back. The stone comes loose, disgorged from the mud with a jolting burst. Only his boots sunk deep in the muck keep him from losing his footing. He takes hold of it now, thumbs the sand and mud from it, peeling it off, the rind of some dark fruit: the yawning eyesockets, the rotted teeth, the sweep of the mandibular arches and forgets to gasp, wonders if his silence comes because the others, all the others, are too far away to hear? And sees that they also, each of them, stands on a mound, each mound separate from the other mounds. *Place of skulls*, he thinks, *Golgotha*, this must be, golcuk, katyn, el mozote, my lai, sabra and shatilla, no gun ri, babi yar, kigali, oradur sûr glane, copiapo, *Golgotha, resurrection of the dead* . . . the dry lake giving up its skulls, so many restless souls with no one to console them, releasing their spirits like moisture, like mist rising from a surface still as glass. . . .

– Viek . . . ? Viek . . . ? Are you done . . . ? Done digging . . . ?

. . . more; more to come, endless . . .

– Viek . . . ?

. . . soweto, grozny, jenin . . . endless; no coming to an end of it . . .

Up to his knees now in the muck . . . losing his footing, falling in the earth that smells of rot . . . he can't get up, not any more. Lies there, still. Still at last. Listens . . . marvels as he listens. Still: nothing in his gut, no rumbling, no bubbling, no welling in his veins, no rushing of the waters . . . and his breath, no roaring in his ears . . . just the whine, the high, thin shriek of his nerves, *eeeeeeeee*, hears it, then that, too, goes still . . .

– Viek . . . ?

And feels himself sinking. He's nodding now, on the point of dozing off, that kind of droning, nodding. If only he could sleep . . . sleep just for a moment . . . .that humming in his ears . . . that hum in the far distance. Closer. Coming closer now. Light. Light, now. A glimmer. *Lights*. Two. Two now. Some vehicle. Some vehicle, must be. Bouncing: headlights. And the motor rumbling. Coming closer. Slits his eyes, shields them from the blinding light, hears the brakes grating, road gravel flying, doors squealing open to either side. Two men jump out. Army fatigues, military boots. He can see them through half closed lids, stamping in the roadbed, slapping at their sides in the red pulse of the taillights, laughing. Now they are bending over him.

– Sheesh, says the one. Deader'n roadkill. Dunno,

Alfie. Looks like it's too late.

  – Get off it. He's probably faking. I know these guys.

  – Hey! Get up!

He sees them plainly now, exhaust from the tailpipe swirling around them, their faces florid in the light. He wishes they would let him sleep.

  – What say?

  – I think he's coming to.

  – Told you: it's the last fucking time.

  – Quit pissing and moaning! Just grab him by the armpits, willya?

He just wants to sleep, warm and comfortable, sleep as if there's no awaking.

  – Hell, no, pal. Not out here.

  – Not on your life. You wanna freeze your sorry ass?

  – Wake up! Lift him up. Higher. *Higher*, ferchrissake!

They have him by the armpits and by the ankles now. Too tired to resist, he feels himself half carried, half swung onto the seat where he lands hard with a thud.

  – That's better.

  – Don'tcha know ya could of froze out there, wearing them thin pajamas . . . ?

  – Hey. Grab some of this. . . .

He feels himself being wrestled to an upright position. A thermos pressed to his lips. Something hot. Bitter. A taste of iron. He wants to spit it out.

  – Drink up.

Awful stuff. He splutters, chokes on half a swallow.

  – Easy, now. Don't want to be messing up our nice new jeep. He feels the other fellow pressing something against his mouth, dry, dry like hardtack. He clamps his jaw tight, tries to shake him off.

  – Hey Smith! Wake up!

Now his eyes are open wide, but they're not addressing him. Despite the obscurity, he makes out someone sitting quietly at the wheel, apparently dozing.

– Ferchrissake, Smith, we ain't got all night. Move it, will ya?

Whoever it is manages to rouse himself, throws the engine into gear, the clutch engages and the vehicle lurches forward. His two rescuers swivel in their seats to get a better look at him. One thumbs the air, pointing toward the driver.

– Guy up front, name's Smith . . .

– He does the driving.

– Yeah. We call him Smith. But he ain't really Smith. He's the chauffeur.

– Yeah. And I'm Alfie, and this here's O'Megan, *semper fidelis*. 'Born to Kill'.

O'Megan elbows Alfie in the ribs.

– Aw, whyn't you just shut up?

– We're Border Patrol.

– Border?

– Yeah. Nothing to worry about, 'ceptin' you just walked through our nice new fence.

He's puzzled. He doesn't remember seeing any fence.

– You din't see no nice big fence out there? Says 'no trespassin'? Come on, we heard you out there *hey,hey,heying*. Trying outcha pipes, hunh? Just don't try blowing the chauffeur.

– Yeah, Smith don't need no one sucking up to him.

Through half-closed eyes he watches them slap each other on the thigh, hears their heaving guffaws, their smacking slaps.

– Lots of folks shit their pants out there, 'specially in the dark. *Hey, hey, hey!* More gasping guffaws, more slapping smacks.

– Yeah. Even Jesus ate it once. *Lamasabacthani.* Know what that is? That's Jew for *hey, hey, hey.* More heaving guffaws, more smacking slaps.

He wishes they would let him sleep. He squeezes his eyes shut tight. Feels them shaking him.

– Hey! Listen up! Know why Jesus din't have no neck?

O'Megan elbows his partner savagely.

– For Chrissake, quit it, Alfie. What's with you, always with the Jesus stuff. How dya know the guy ain't sheeny?

– Jeez, why you always so up tight? You want equal time or what? O.K. Listen: here's one: why is Jesus and all Jewboys alike?

He checks the urge to frown. *Swampdwellers*. They're nothing if not persistent. They would do better to let him sleep.

– Give up?

– Give up?

He shrugs, half obligingly, half in resignation.

– See? O'Megan nudges Alfie. I told ya.

– But he don't look like no yid!

– O.K., give up?

He sits quietly, determined to say nothing.

– Because they live at home till they're 30 . . .

– they take over their father's business . . .

– *AND THEIR MOTHERS THINK THEY'RE GOD!*

He can barely watch them, slapping their knees, falling all over themselves laughing. In the excitement one even passes gas. He shuts his eyes.

– Hey! says O'Megan, grabbing at his elbow and shaking. Hey! Ain't no time to fall asleep. Just cause Alfie here tried gassing us to death!

– Fuck you, O'Megan! It was you cut it!

– Was not!

– Was, so! Show a little respect, for Chrisssake.

His eyes drift shut.

– Hey! Here's one: You know – when they cut it off? – what they call a sheeny foreskin? Give up? Give up?

– A lamp shade! Get it? Get it? Hunh? I don't think he gets it.

– Cut the shit, says O'Megan.

– What's eatin' you? Fuck, man, mellow out! See, O'Megan and me, we're real tight, we just like our little joke, hunh, Smith?

He has almost forgotten the driver, but now his name is mentioned, in the briefest instant it comes to him: *the Land Rover driver!* same cap, same expression, still chewing gum. Automatically, his hand reaches for the map he remembers extracting from the dead man's pocket. Smith checks his gesture in the rearview mirror. He turns around.

– Forget something?

– See, didn't I tell you: Smith here knows everything, only he don't let nothing on.

For a moment he hesitates. He would like to ignore them.

– Just my orders.

Everything turns very quiet. He is conscious now of the hum of the engine. They look at him. O'Megan reaches out a hand.

– Give 'em here.

Reluctantly, he works his orders free from his breast pocket. Alfie looks them over before passing them to O'Megan.

– Here, Pops, you be the judge.

O'Megan studies them. He shakes his head.

– Unsigned like this? Piss on 'em! Wouldn't pass muster. Not even in hell. They prob'ly won't let you through. O'Megan flashes him a toothy smile.

– Hey! Smith! Alfie alerts the driver, better keep this one out of the salvage yard!

– Yeah.

– Take him round the back way. Delivery entrance. More heaving guffaws, more smacking slaps. Explosive hoots that make him shudder. And he can't shut out their steaming breath, *dog's breath*, it comes to him, the stink of spoiling meat. He turns his gaze away.

For a time the vehicle hums along a road bordering a cyclone fence. He cranes his neck to see. Can it be this is the fence they meant? Although the windows are fogged over now, when he rubs the steam away, he can make out great piles of scrap metal, oil drums and abandoned car parts. At last Smith swings to the left, and pulls up at what appears to be a guard post. A sentry steps forward into the glare of the headlights.

– Security, he barks.

Out of the darkness a decontamination crew appears, their faces hidden behind respirators. One of them wheels something beneath the undercarriage, others pass their lead-gloved hands over the contours of the chassis, palpating every surface. What are they searching for, he wonders? The motor idles, steam rises from the exhaust. He strains to see outside. As the sentry withdraws the detection apparatus, he makes out a kind of animal mounted on it, white, nearly formless – like a slug, but white, with stunted arms and legs – a creature, man, perhaps, curled as a homunculus, chained to the device, small enough to slide beneath any undercarriage, no matter how low slung, and he swears he sees it weep, but perhaps this is merely a reflection of the light in its unusually bright eyes.

– All clear! The sentry waves their vehicle through.

O'Megan throws him a sharp look.

– Looks like Pee-Wee din't find nothin! Ain't you the lucky stiff!

More knee slaps, more sickening guffaws. The driver rolls up the window. Once more, they are on their way. At last the vehicle grinds to a halt behind a line of taxis in a drafty underpass. Overhead, banners snap noisily in the breezeway. A liveried doorman stoops to swing the passenger door open. Alfie rolls down the curbside window, suddenly all smiles.

– Hey, Peters! Long time no see. What's cooking, blood?

– All right! Hey, dude, gimme some skin! Whatchu bring me some passenger? They seem to know one another, all back slaps, and easy affability.

The doorman stands ramrod straight, waiting for him to step onto the curb. His legs are cramped. He slides one foot out, then the other, slowly stretches himself upright.

– O.K., the doorman barks, slamming the door shut

behind him.

     – So long now. Alfie waves.

     – Enjoy your stay, O'Megan calls out with a great guffaw.

     The vehicle pulls away from the curb, trailing the echo of their laughter, a blossom of exhaust in its wake. He stands shivering on the pavement watching it, relieved to see it go. He tries to keep his pajama top from flapping open. The doorman turns to him almost as an afterthought.

     – Wait here, man, I gotta get a dolly.

     – A dolly?

     – Yeah.

     – There's no need really. I don't have any bags.

     – Regulations, man. We wheel you in here. And when you leave, we wheel you out.

     Alone now, he marks time in the reception area, drumming his fingers mechanically on the dusty surface of the receiving desk, observing how the lobby is narrow and dimly lit, the entire foyer paneled in some dark wood, oak probably, or mahogany. In the obscurity of the hallway he can barely make out open bags of cement stacked against the walls. Repairs must be in progress. He props his elbows on the counter, waiting. The lobby clock reads midnight. Later, when he happens to glance again, he realizes the hands have moved only slightly. But now they read three minutes to twelve.

     At last he thinks he hears someone coming. The reception door squeals open. One pushing, one pulling, two starched and uniformed chamber maids struggle with a heavy refuse bin mounted on casters. They pant and grunt, yanking it this way and that, through a door which is clearly much too narrow. When they catch sight of him, they straighten up.

     – Oops! Sorry! We weren't expecting anyone this late. Almost in tandem, they adjust their caps and pat their white cleaning uniforms in place.

     – When did you come in?

     – Just now.

Their bafflement doesn't seem strange to him. After all, he has arrived unannounced.

– Smith brought me, he adds as an afterthought.

– Smith? They look at one another, scrunching up their noses.

– In the jeep, he explains.

– Oh, you're the one! The blonde one giggles coquettishly. Of course! They told us about you!

– I think there may be some mistake. There's no way anyone here could know I would be coming. I didn't know myself.

The dark one appraises him.

– Then you're not Joe Viek?

Somehow her expression makes him want to offer reassurance.

– Well, yes, as a matter of fact, he flashes her a winning smile, but I'm probably not *that* Joe Viek.

His small attempt at humor has little apparent effect. The dark one's tone turns suddenly insistent, almost accusatory.

– But that's your name, isn't it?

– Well, yes. But I'm just not the Viek you heard about. No one here's expecting me.

The blonde exchanges a look with her companion.

– Oh! By the way: my name's Magda, and this (she simpers at her dark companion) this here is Mary, your hostess for the night.

– Hostess?

– Well, yes! Everyone's assigned a hostess. She drops a little curtsey. Especially if you plan on staying for a while.

– No, no, he reassures them, I'm just here for the night.

– Unhunh, says Mary, nodding knowingly. I'll just go fix up your room.

He makes a move to follow, but the blonde one, the one named Magda, catches him by the elbow, all insinuating smiles.

    – Wait! Mary's pretty careless sometimes . . . She lowers her voice, do you have your things?

    – Things? He stares at her mystified.

    – You know: things . . . with you . . . for the night.

    Although her tone strikes him as quite intimate, he has no idea what things she might refer to.

    – Then I guess I'll have to get you some. She throws him a suggestive look.

    She is gone for some time. He leans his elbows against the reception counter. The plastic bin remains behind the counter where they seem to have forgotten it. Something prompts him to reach out and raise the lid. Someone is crouched inside, motionless, apparently asleep. The crown of his bald head glows a sudden pink in the overhead light. A snore or two escapes him before he starts up with a snort.

    – Oh, excuse me! I didn't see you there! I'm a little hard of hearing anyway. I'm terribly sorry. You're probably waiting for your key. He strains to reach an overhead peg board from which dangles an ancient key.

    – But no one's given me a room assignment yet!

    – That's not a problem! Could you just reach it for me up there . . . ? I have trouble standing up. And you need to sign the book. Could I trouble you to step in here behind the counter? There's a half-door to the right.

    The hour is late. He is happy to oblige. He swings the low door ajar.

    – It's somewhere on one of these shelves back here. Yes. Down there. That's right. Could you hand it to me?

    He bends down. One by one, he slides the enormous ledgers out far enough to read their titles.

    – No! No! Not that one! That one stays where it is! The desk clerk's voice takes on a sudden hint of rage.

    When he turns around, he is surprised to see the night clerk sitting in a motorized wheel chair, his legs and feet shrouded in a carriage blanket.

– Excuse me. I didn't mean to be short. You see, those are just the account books. What you want is the guest book. There. That's the one. Just sign the page where the signatures run out.

– But what about the painting?

– What painting?

– The painting here! "The Mystic Lamb." The tryptich by van Eyck. Take a look! He struggles to slide the tome across the counter for the clerk to see.

– Oh, that old thing? Don't worry. It's probably just a copy. Nobody will notice anyway! Just sign your name underneath the others. Anywhere will do.

He inscribes his name as carefully as the clerk's chancy pen allows.

– Check! The clerk folds the leaves and heaves the triptych shut.

– Czech? Close, but not exactly: Russian.

– Russian! We don't get many of them down here. Viek, hunh? What's it mean?

– A hundred years.

– That's a good one! Mr. Century, eh?

– You might say.

– Good. Now here's your key. You're all set. Number twenty. He glances over his shoulder. Just between you and me, we have so much to do. None of us can ever keep up. The management runs us ragged, day and night, night and day. And it's getting worse. There s no place left to catch even forty winks. I have to hide in the refuse bin. And the damn clock always stalls, the waste disposers aren't worth a damn, the drains always clog . . . . Nothing works! I keep telling them to flush them, but of course they never do. They're even thinking of shutting down the swimming pool. I don't know if I can stand it here much longer. I'm seriously thinking of giving notice – I know you'll keep all this in the strictest confidence. Of course, if I give notice, there goes my pension, and there's the little matter of finding other work, and just now there's

only the one opening. He lowers his voice. They need someone
to load the meat truck and at my age, I'm not suited to heavy
lifting anymore. I know I shouldn't be burdening you with my
problems. They dismiss you at once if you complain – and I
was such a rebel once! Well, enough of that! Could I trouble
you to wait by the elevator? The girl will be down any second.
He drops his voice below a whisper: Which one did you get?
Maggie or the dark one?

      He decides to ignore what he takes to be a tasteless
question. All he really wants is sleep. He feels a pulsing in his
head, and his footsteps, grating on the cement particles litter-
ing the hallway, seem to him unusually loud. The air is drafty,
and he detects a trace of stale urine. He presses the call button. There seems to be no response. He waits, leaning his
weight against the wall opposite the lift, thinking of nothing,
nearly dozing off.

      A painful grating, a churning of gears awakens his
attention. Antique cables crackle as the elevator descends.
When the cage finally comes into view, it seems to be empty, at
least at first, but when he slides the gate open, he discovers
Magda, one leg cocked seductively, half reclining on the
leather banquette, her starched cap slightly askew. She slides
her skirt up past her thighs. He notices the dark invitation
between her legs.

      – Don't tell Mary, she purrs, we're just about ready!
      – Won't someone notice?
      – Bashful, aren't you! Her red lips curl with sarcasm.
Anyway, I'm not done yet for the night. I just wanted to make
sure you got your things. Here you are: soap; toothbrush;
cream . . . .She smiles flirtatiously. She straightens her cap
and adjusts her skirt before stepping out into the corridor. I'll
come check on you later. Let's see where the night clerk put
you . . . ?

      He fumbles in his pocket for the key. She scratches at
the number with a practiced finger.

      – Twenty! That old devil. I can't believe he gave you

20! It's been sealed up since the accident! Oh, never mind! I'll
catch up with you later. Now don't run away!

He waits for her to disappear down the hall before
sliding the gate closed. He allows himself to slump exhausted
on the banquette, accidentally knocking soap, comb and
toothpaste to the floor. He picks them up. He presses 2. At
first nothing happens. He re-examines his key. The number is
clearly engraved on the shaft: 20. He tries 2 again. This time
the mechanism gives a sudden lurch, but the cage, instead of
rising, sinks slowly just past the basement level where it settles
with a sigh. He can't suppress the urge to laugh. Hitting bottom. Here he is: a key to nowhere, trapped at the bottom of the
shaft. Well, well, it's probably just as well. The room upstairs
is boarded anyway – unless of course the girl is lying. He wonders briefly what may have happened there. He imagines some
kind of surgical procedure, chrome retractors, someone drawing breath under the anesthesiologist's mask, the black rubber
bag inflating, deflating. *Ten, nine, eight, seven* . . . .He shakes
the image from his mind. Overactive imagination, probably
just fatigue. Apply upstairs for another room. He searches for
the lobby button, but there doesn't seem to be one. He tries
pressing one number after another. Nothing happens; the lift
seems to be permanently stuck. He considers shouting, but at
this hour, he would probably disturb the other guests. The
idea comes to him why not make his bed in here? The banquette, although it feels rather rigid, seems quite long enough
to accommodate him fairly comfortably. He has everything he
needs, toothbrush, comb . . . . And at this level the shaft is
enclosed, ensuring a night of privacy.

About to stretch out, he discovers there's even a dis-
posable shaver. Except someone has removed the blade.
Amusing. If he were inclined to do away with himself, he could
always attach his pajama drawstring to the overhead light – if
he had a drawstring. If there were a light. Even more amusing.
He stretches out on the banquette. He will puzzle out the prob-
lem in theory: a shaver without a blade, a bar of soap, a comb,

a toothbrush. In what permutation or combination might any of these things present fatal opportunities? He could (for example) slip on the soap, causing him to fall and impale himself on the comb – if the comb were held just so. But if he is to be preoccupied falling, he has to have an extra hand to immobilize the comb, and in any case, such a clumsy scheme hardly offers a suitable demise for a man in his . . . in his . . . and besides he feels an insistent pressure now in his bladder . . . .

He catches sight of the industrial door opener. Suddenly he is on his feet. He seizes hold of the leather strap, pulls on it with all his weight. Slowly the massive jaws slide open to reveal a brightly lit subbasement, a utility area, probably. Nothing along the corridor but industrial steel doors. The passageway is deserted, but then at this hour, who would he expect to see? A janitor, perhaps, come to stoke the furnace? He pads along the hallway, trying one doorknob after another. He comes on a convenient recess. No one would notice if he were to . . .

– Pst. Pst! Mary, the dark one, signals to him from behind a fire door half ajar. Naughty boy! She waves a warning finger at him. I thought you'd never make it! What took you so long? Now there's nowhere left. Every single mattress is taken. What a drag! I'll have to put you up in the crawl space. And it's so dark in there. Hang on just a minute while I go get us some light!

She ducks behind the fire door. Moments later she reappears, a burning candle in hand. She guides him down a long corridor until they come to an opening behind a stairwell. She motions him inside a low passage between the interior wall and the foundation.

– Duck, she warns him. It's dark in here, but they keep it pretty clean. The only trouble is we have to be very quiet so we don't bother them next door.

He begins to hear loud voices coming from behind the wall.

– Who's that making such a racket? Most of the guests

must be asleep by now.

— Not these folks. They're rehearsing. They have to work all night because in the daytime the room is occupied by someone else. She spreads a bed roll on the concrete. Here, try this, she says.

He searches for a place to put his things.

— Oh, just drop them on the floor. Anywhere will do. They'll be quite safe. No one comes in here unl . . .

The rest of her words are lost in the white folds of her uniform as she disrobes. He watches her drop the spaghetti-thin straps of her black lace teddy, watches it drop past her nipples . . . . She unhooks her garter belt and stretches out on the bedroll next to him. She begins to fondle him, warming to her task. Despite his fatigue, he feels his blood begin to rise. She edges closer to him.

— Mmmmm. I like it here, don't you? Slowly she unrolls his waist band. She slides a practiced hand downward, toward his sex.

— I love it down here. And with all the reflector stars glued up on the ceiling, it's so romantic. It's supposed to be a star map of Cygnus-in-Capricorn, but it's really a rogue galaxy. Here, make yourself useful. Take some of this stuff and dab it on my lips. She sits up in bed, groping for a tube of salve.

— It's just like in a real theater, except of course they can't see you, but you can hear every word. And it doesn't cost anything. Later, when they're ready, they'll be appearing in the firehouse. And you should see the actors! They all wear wigs just like in court. But they're not real wigs, of course. They make them out of that black spaghetti.

He is not sure what she means.

— You know: that kind of rubber tubing . . . ? They use it on the detainees so it won't leave any marks.

— And they use the same stuff to make wigs?

— Oh, sure! They recycle it. And the actors really love it.

— I can't imagine why.

– It helps them get into the part.

From time to time as he moistens her sex he makes out fragments of conversation. Quite distinctly. Someone calling. A sharp scream.

– *Miep! Miep!*

– *Shhh. They'll hear you downstairs. It's just a bad dream she's having.*

– *Mother, they're coming to take us . . .*

– *It's Anne, darling. She's having a bad dream. Go to sleep: it's just a bad dream.*

Mary's voice sounds husky in his ear.

– Listen! That's Rachel Lebowski. You know: the famous actress. She's nearly seventy years old! She couldn't get a part for years, now they have her playing Anne Frank!

– But she must be a detainee.

– Not so loud! You'll distract them. Everyone here's a detainee, she smiles. They're just the actor-detainees.

– Is there a difference?

– Actors always think they're somewhere else.

– And the others?

– Oh, the others know. Come now, don't look so glum. Mary's gonna make nice. It's not so bad: they wheel you in here and in the end, they wheel you out.

He feels her tongue worm its way around his cock.

The actors in the next room are still at it, their voices suddenly uncomfortably loud.

– *Come on, I'm waiting. Take off your shirt.*

– *They're going to beat us!*

– *No, no, please. Not me. Him, there. Him. He can take it. Not me!*

– *Open the door!*

He hears their threats give way to arpeggios of stagy laughter. Mary has him by the shoulders, shaking him.

– Get up! They're just about ready.

He rubs his eyes.

– Come on! We have to hurry.

He catches sight of Magda sweeping his things up from the concrete.

– Don't touch those. Leave my things alone!

The bar of soap falls out of Magda's grasp and explodes in tiny fragments. He feels a sharp sting. He glances at his exposed leg, at the dark trickle inching its way along his shank. He takes it up with a swipe of his finger, but when he licks it, he discovers his blood tastes of iron. Mary eyes him reproachfully.

– We have no time to waste. She stands to one side, all discipline, forcing him to pass. Magda leads, groping her way along the crawl space. Mary pushes him to his knees.

– Keep down! It's best not to let them see you.

He crawls forward till they come to an opening in the wall where someone must have knocked the plaster out. He crouches, straining to see. Inside is a giant swimming pool. High intensity lights hang overhead. Thousands of swimmers, all naked, stand in the water up to their waists. Many more are lined up on the runways. Behind them, uniformed guards swing their truncheons, forcing groups of swimmers to leap into the water. On the loading dock, a road crew is straining to tip over an enormous vat, pouring something grey and viscous into the pool. Quite close to him, one of the bathers, a young girl, catches sight of him peering at her. She crosses her thin arms, hiding the small rose nubs on her chest.

– That's Rachel Lebowski! Can you believe it? Seventy years old and she's so immersed in her role, she's developed young girl's breasts.

The actress seems to be waving at him now, or perhaps she is stretching her thin arms out to him.

– Please, mister. Please. Please get me out. It burns, it burns so badly.

– Don't mind her, Mary whispers. With the new polymers, they can pave over the pool so fast, no one hardly feels a thing.

He watches the girl lose her footing and slide beneath

the surface. Magda pulls him away from the opening.

– If they see you, it just makes it worse.

– But someone must know this is going on!

In the reflected light he sees Mary's mouth harden.

– Did you have someone in mind?

– But there must be someone, a lifeguard or the manager, perhaps.

– The manager! Mary begins to laugh. He can see her soft palate vibrating, her laugh coming at him louder and louder. He feels himself swept in the enormous hollow of her mouth, unable to stop himself, sucked in by the air currents of a gaping tunnel. A piercing whistle alerts him. Steel rails glint in the headlights of an oncoming train. Just in time, he presses his back against the wall. The train streaks by. It is packed with travellers. Rush hour, he thinks, but then he sees that inside they are all naked, some of them crying, others wailing and screaming. A young girl peers through a soiled window, her mouth wide, her lips flattened against the pane. He can hear her piercing shrieks disappearing down the tracks.

A smell comes to him, a smell of burning. Another car streams by filled with people whose skin seems to be smoldering. There must be hundreds of them. On fire. How can they pack them in so tight? And someone is shouting, shouting something. It must be him, he thinks he recognizes his voice shouting, but the roar of the tunnel is too loud, too overwhelming. Nobody could hear him. He cannot hear himself.

He stumbles backwards. Before he can stop himself, his foot kicks over something in the dark.

– *Scheisse! Idiot!* Can't you watch where you put your feet? A crunching blow to his groin sinks him to the ground. He touches something foul. Something foul and wet and sticky.

He tries to sit up. He is surrounded by ashen grey men, thinner than death, convulsed in silent laughter, bones showing under their skin, all in pajamas. Striped. Like his. Exactly like his. Others line the walls, lying belly down, stacked three to a bunk, craning their necks, spectators eager for a fight.

– Come on, make him lick it up! Someone twists his neck in an armlock, smashes his head against a bunk post. With a sudden burst of light, a utility hatch swings open. Between the tracks, a man stands, helmetted, in protective clothing, his face, his hulk grotesque in the light reflected from below.

– For the love of God, can't we have one single, frigging, solitary game in here without you assholes always kicking up a fuss? Knock it off, willya? Can'tcha see everyone's gone home?

The hatch slams shut. But even in the dark, even suited and helmetted, the man's silhouette is monstrous. Unmistakable. It's the driver. It's Smith. He's sure of it. Smith again. The vehicle must be nearby.

– Smith! he shouts. Wait!

But Smith doesn't answer. The reflector bands of his lineman's uniform glow pearly in the thick air of the subway tunnel. He is moving down the way, dipping and raising his foreman's lantern, tapping at the rails, methodically checking the rivets. Now and again the tracks ring out with the blow of his lineman's hammer.

– Wait up!

He stumbles along, trying to catch up to him, but the tracks are dark, the going difficult. He keeps tripping over the ties in the obscurity. In the growing distance he can still make out Smith's lantern bobbing, its rays casting their glint now and again on the empty tracks.

What does he expect? A lift perhaps to some friendlier destination? Smith is just a name. It could be the name of any driver, like Mack, or Jack – or Joe. He smiles wryly to himself.

Deep in the tunnel, a cobalt lamp signals an emergency telephone. He must be close to a station. In the dimness he makes out a stark white bed. As he approaches, he discovers someone lying there. A girl. He bends over her, studying her features. When he lifts the sheet, he discovers she is naked. Involuntarily a gasp escapes him: her pubescent body gives off a cobalt glow, phosphorescent in the light. He watches her thin chest heaving faintly, laboring for breath.

Why is her face familiar? He has seen her somewhere before: the straight dark hair spread out now on the pillow, the white barrette, and her eyebrows, their troubled slant arching upward above the nose. No. Anne Frank would have to be at least seventy years old. And this girl . . . he stares at her rosebud breasts. Where has he seen her? Was it in the swimming pool, sliding under the waters? Can she still be breathing? And yet he detects the distinct rise and fall of her chest. Comatose, perhaps, the brain deprived of oxygen. He is reluctant to wake her, mesmerized by the blue nubs of her breasts, rising, falling.

– Rachel? *Rachel Lebowski?*

Is he expecting perhaps to see her eyelids flutter? He wonders if his whisper can rouse her. If only he could listen to her heart. Absent his instruments, he will have to brace himself, one hand propped against each side of the thin mattress. He rests his head against her chest. Lub, dup, lub, dup. Diastole. Sistole. He can make her heartbeat out quite distinctly. Distinctly normal. Nothing to give cause for alarm. A narrow chest, a young girl's chest, the raised flesh of the soft areola trembling with each beat. He imagines what his hair must feel like, brushing against her skin. Will her eyelids flicker?

– *Rachel?*

Something distracts his attention. He straightens up. A blonde woman is standing next to him. She seems cool, unconcerned in her fur hat.

– Could you tell me? When is the next train to Prypiat?

Hanging directly above him, he notices a clock with four faces. Each reads precisely twelve. My god, why hadn't he realized it before? This must be the central station! All these people, rushing, heels rapping against the marble, hauling suitcases, huge bundles wrapped in burlap, wheeling bales of merchandize on trolleys, pushing trunks across the marble

floor. Lines everywhere. People running, frantic to be on their
way.

    The woman is growing insistent.

    – The next train? I need to go to Prypiat.

    My god, she must have seen. Watched his every move.
Could she have seen him lift the sheet, bend to listen to the
patient's heart, seen him sink his face against her naked
breasts? Perhaps when she's not looking he'll cover the
patient's face with the sheet . . . .He licks his fingers, thumb-
ing through the stationmaster's ledger . . .

    – The next train to Prypiat . . . ?

IMMEDIATE DEPARTURE. LEAVING ON TRACK TWELVE . . .

The loudspeaker's echo is swallowed by the sound of running
feet, the grating of trunks being dragged across the floor.

    . . . or better still, slide her farther down in her hospi-
tal bed . . .

. . . TRACK TWELVE FOR IMMEDIATE DEPARTURE

    He pulls at her ankles until her feet touch the chipped
enamel footrail, but when he goes to pull the sheet over her
face, spread out on the pillow, he discovers fallen clumps of
her dark hair, like the wings of a dead bird, severed at the
roots. On the sheet a stain appears, spreading on the surface.
He can make it out quite plainly, but he can't do anything to
stop her fever. Suddenly he remembers the train schedule.

    – Prypiat . . . Prypiat . . . he licks his finger, thumb-
ing through the pages. Here it is! Next one leaves at twelve.

    But the woman is gone. No one appears to notice him.
They are all running to catch the train.

O-N- -T-I-M-E- -D-E-P-A-R-T-U-R-E- -O-N- -T-I-M-E- -D-E-
Beneath a band of rolling type, a clock reads precisely twelve.

WATCH THE DOORS!

They are running frenziedly now, shoving each other out of the way, frantic to hurl themselves at the closing doors. The electronic monitor tracks a man in the far distance running along the platform.

– *Watch out! Can't you see where you're going?*

The camera zooms in on a bystander. Methodically he puts the runner's eye out with a knife. The image, vastly magnified, is projected on the departure bulletin where the swarming crowds watch as the man's iris is expelled, gelatinous as an eggyolk to the sound of roaring laughter. Beneath, a line of type rolls out

P-R-Y-P-I-A-T- -P-R-Y-P-I-A-T- -P-R-Y-P-I-A-T- -P-R-Y-P-I-

He watches, momentarily distracted, but when he turns back to the patient he discovers the stain smoldering, its dark ring gaping wider. At any moment, someone is bound to see it eating through the sheet. He squats inside the information booth, under the illuminated clock that reads midnight. He lifts the sheet. Under it, the patient's chest cavity yawns, charred and smoking – exactly in the place where, earlier, he bent his head to listen to her heart.

– Stop it, for God's sake, he whispers, can't you stop it?

He feels wave after wave of heat, rising. The blonde woman is there, standing behind the counter.

– Six, he babbles, six. The train to Priapyt . . . the next one leaves at six.

STAND BACK! CLOSE THE DOORS!

He presses his hand hard against the swelling in his groin. The woman begins to laugh. Peals of laughter echo in the cavernous hollow of the station. The station clock whirs.

The minute hand jerks. One minute past midnight. Suddenly all motion ceases. People are standing frozen, stunned. They are staring at the information booth. At him. Slowly the surveillance camera scans the room. It locks on the information booth, zooms in on him, on the woman laughing, on the patient's image projected now on the departure bulletin, magnified one hundred times, the dark lotus of her rib cage bursting open as the flame consumes her from the inside out. People stand in small groups, transfixed, watching, their faces illuminated in the fire that licks at her thin extremities, reaching outward for her face, her feet, exploding when it strikes her hair.

– Viek! Aren't you Joseph Viek . . . ?

He feels a hand clamping his shoulder.

– Your time is up.

And opens his eyes. And stares into the night watchman's face and what he took to be some Rastafarian with his dreads, smiles at him benevolently, transformed now in the slanting rays of dawn: shining blonde curls, white, Dresden-white skin, eyes nearly colorless, orbs translucent like gems, and sees himself reflected in the sharpness of their pupils, and within their depths sees the double doors swing wide behind him and light! Light, streaming radiant, nearly blinding with a luminosity he can't imagine ever having seen before.

And hears the watchman's voice: your time is up. The night is over. Day has come at last. The doors have opened. And sees the throng of people leaning against the barricades, straining against the security tape, and the gendarmes maintaining perfunctory decorum. His relatives: there they are, all of them, all there, waving, waving to him: Viek! A great shout goes up. Yussef! Jozef! Joe! Jose! All there, all his village, every one of them, and they sweep him up in their arms, raise him on their shoulders, and take him, carry him, streaming toward the waiting curb, and pile into taxis, slam doors, whoop with glee, and there's the town players, all the Rom, with their great basses, violins and zithers in the flatbed, waiting to sing him home, and they fly over ribbons of asphalt, past the reflecting glass of the great silent towers, speeding over the raised roadways, weaving under, over, and under again, past signs he doesn't recognize – where has he been? – and lights, whole strings of lights, and he hears them singing, and the violins scraping against the great rush of wind, and senses Myrna, Myrna unwinding his woolen scarf, and pulling him close, and feels her tears wet against his cheek. *Moya, moya chubish*, he whispers, where have you been? and he feels his brows smoothe flat, shedding their years, the slump of weight lifted, and he soars, he flies, and the streets of the suburbs streak by, and now the road runs through open country, meadowlands, and now the fields burst into green, waves of grass, fanned by the wind; and he watches birds flushed from the tops of trees, hears their panicked cries signalling their approach, and sweeps past the whirl of leaves, a green whirlwind, and feels the earth churning, spinning, and he hears now the great song, the song of the Rom pounding their zithers, and the taxi bounces over the rough stretches, and the driver curses the shocks, and his father turns around in the front seat: *Jozef, you're home at last!* And he sits at the long white table in the yard filled with long white tables, their white spreads all but hidden under the weight of red, and green and purple fruit and the black seeds of the caviar, and tips a shot of fire water to his lips. And reaches for another slug, and passes each platter along, one by one to his neighbor, and Myrna sits by him, and lifts her bundled arms around him, and he plays at pushing her away, and pulls at her scarf to bring her close again, and smells her neck, her dizzying smell, half roses, half the musky scent of slept-in hair, and loves, and loves and loves. And Mammo brings him her best pigeon pie, and offers him the knife, and his mother smiles at him beneath her combs, the jeweled combs she loves to wear, and the Rom lead the courtyard with their dance, and everyone begins to clap, and he smacks his hands against the table, and feels the blood coming to the surface, the tingling, and he smacks and smacks harder,

and he laughs and laughs. He wants to keep this moment, to
hold it: the music, the whirling shawls, their bright fringes
whipping the air, the stomping feet, the clapping, the song rising from every throat, wants to hold on to it forever . . .

He is behind a window, watching, some place behind a
bush, or sitting on the porch perhaps, now the weather has
thawed, and the apple trees have burst into bloom, whitening
the countryside in their confetti of new snow, watching, watching the village come to life – it's the village of his childhood,
where he was born – but he is an old man now – sees his mother hanging the sheets, flapping them in the spring chill, swinging the far ends over the rope, hears her groan a little as she
reaches higher than her natural stretch, sees her worry the
clothespin against the damp, hears the sheets' slight squeal as
the pin bites into the line, watches her, sees her bend and
stretch: the dance, always the dance of his mother, swinging
her basket on the way to market, gossiping with auntie over
the garden fence; pulling the leeks for soup, stirring the big
iron pot over the blackened stove, packing it with newspaper,
her red hair ringed in fire. And his father in his shop, miter-
ing the hinges, detailing, planing the rough wood into submis-
sion, watches his large work-gnarled hands pull finishing nails
small as fish bones from between his teeth, position them firm-
ly, strike them home with two smart hammer blows *(that's why
we called you Jozef, that you, too, might be a carpenter)*, listens to his mother's stories as she tucks him in, sits at the edge
of his feather bed, raises his fevered head to drink, from his
sickbed window sees the gooseboy driving the geese to pasture,
flapping at them with his bamboo rod, their shimmer of white
fingering the meadow before they drop below the rise and
hears them honking and splashing in the pond. And hears the
chatter of women in the washhouse, and remembers the first
time they didn't let him watch, and learned about burials. And
how they filed out from the Old Believer's church, and up into
the hills, to the graveyard, he and all the others: the old men,
and the children, and their mothers sniffling, wiping their

noses in great homespun handkerchiefs, and the children running wild, and the old metropolitan with his easter bread hat,
swaying, whispering prayers for the dead *(what's he saying,
mother?)* and remembering her shuushhhh. And running with
Otar and Susana to the river in the soft summer morning, and
casting their little lines, hoping, hoping for the trout that
never came *(I got one! Look! I got one!)* and envying the size,
and the triumph, and seeing its pink mouth gasping for
breath, lace-edged with tiny teeth, and its gills laboring:
knights' magic armor, breast plates, mail, scaled, silver, per-
fect, iridescent in sunlight. And running, running bare legged
through the fields so everyone could see, imagining that he, he
too, and Susana, all of them had caught it. And vowing that he
too would get his turn. And bunching his school books togeth-
er with a strap, and eating the sugar buns his mother slipped
into his knapsack, eating them one by one, long before lunch,
in the morning early on his walk to school, *(wait till I tell
mother on you)* and Mischa, his black dog, shadowing them to
the porch of the wooden schoolhouse, and throwing pebbles
and stones at her to make her go back home, and secretly wish-
ing she could come inside with him and learn to read. And
remembering her smell, wet and metallic when she went swimming with them, and the creek, how it boiled over in the sun,
and how they splashed each other in the cool water, and how
he loved Susana then, saw her thin legs thrashing in the water,
and her nakedness. And imagined how he would kiss her and
what his hands would do, and spread them out both of them
on the grass of his nightdreams *(susana, susana, susana)*,
until he wished he had her name, and wondered if he ever ran
beneath the rainbow would he turn into a woman. And his
father dressing him in his first suit, and lacing up his first city-
dweller's shoes because it's his time to be confirmed, *(today
you are a man)*, and remembering the sunlight, the gold of the
meadow ablaze with buttercups, the cries of mothers in the
soft twilight calling, calling, calling the names of children:
Kirill, Sasha, Mischa, Yatsek, calling them home, the day is

over, and thinking: it was paradise.

And hands raise him from the Watchman's bed: sweep the rough sheets away, and he feels his limbs naked in the cooler air, and feels them rush him through the doors, out of the terminal ward at last. Free, free, free he is at last, free in the light, and they are running with him, running down the way of an ancient corridor, and out into the light and he sees them all; they are all there: Myrna, and Mammo and his mother, and Otar, and his father; and his uncles and aunties; and the children, and all the people of Prypiat, and Brixton, and the blind ones of Bhopal, and the people of Sudan running in their worn clothes, still with the road dust powdering their arms and legs, and all of them are running, running with him, holding him, raising him higher, and he wants to laugh and shout, and ask them where they are going; slow down, slow down, he wants to tell them but they don't hear, they are running, running, and he wonders: is he sick? is he dying? and remembers his mother holding his head as he retches in the privy, and feels the cool of her hand on his forehead, and the clasp of her arm, and vomits, vomits all of it: the short wave, and his instruments, and the apple, and his change of clothes, and his backpack, and the newspaper, and the bill with its watchful eye, his wristwatch, his shoes and belt, and the clothes hanging on the hook, the striped pajamas, and the combs, all of them, and the silver brush, and Anne Frank's costume and her wig, and Mary's black lace teddy, and the tube of salve, all of it, all of it, he can't stop, and his mother praying – for him? – holding his head, and his orders and his passport, and spits his world out backwards from the very last to the very first, and knows he must be about to die and that he must still be very young, can't be more than two or three – his mother, barely nineteen – until there is nothing left to vomit, and still it comes. And hears her voice, the one he knows above all others, hears her pray – is it for him? for him? and hears her voice distinctly, *tut omens, tut animaes, tut creats, tut ter, cant oms, cant ciel e ter, tut cantem gloria,* praying for him, and can't make out the words, and knows that he is dying. And there's Lipsey and Chernoff dressed for All Saints in angel costumes, for god's sake, and the road inspectors in frilly maid's caps, fishnet stockings, organza aprons and silver wands, dancing the cancan, tossing confetti, and the corks pop, and people scream as the bubbly crests the rims, and balloons soar into the midnight sky and brush like sad moths against the flaking ceiling with its fading silver stars, and they are shouting, singing strains of Auld Lang Syne, and fireworks burst, rockets scythe the air, and he hears the distant thunder, the whistling of roman candles, the faint report: swish, swish. BOOM! and sees the glint of constellations: Orion, Capricorn and the Great Bear, party decorations, and strobes shooting their beams from star to star, hears the throb of music, sees the tiny strings of minute particles playing at the heart of things, the dark hum of the universe, and wishes he were home.

About the Author

Bardo99, Cecile Pineda's fifth published book of fiction, presents the 20th century as a character. Both *Bardo99* and *Redoubt*, soon to be published by Wings, are composed in the form of mononovels, that is, novels which are located inside one protagonist's consciousness. *Bardo99* is patterned on the comotose state of the writer's collaborator, actor, and close friend, Thomas Macaulay, who died of AIDS in 1989.

Pineda's published novels include *The Love Queen of the Amazon*, written with the support of a NEA Fiction Fellowship, and named Notable Book of the Year by the New York Times; *Frieze*, set in Ninth Century India and Java; and *Face*, which was nominated for an American Book Award. *Face* received the Gold Medal from the Commonwealth Club of California, and the Sue Kaufman Prize, awarded by the American Academy and Institute of Arts & Letters. Her most recent novel is *Fishlight: A Dream of Childhood* (Wings, 2001). *Redoubt*, a meditation on gender, will be published by Wings Press in the near future, along with new editions of her earlier novels, *Face* and *Frieze*. Pineda teaches creative writing in the San Francisco-Bay Area.

For more information on Cecile Pineda, visit
her webpage at http://www.home.earthlink.net/~cecilep

About the cover artist

Kathy Vargas is an internationally praised artist/photographer whose numerous exhibitions include one-person shows at Sala Uno in Rome and the Galeria San Martín in Mexico City. A major retrospective of Vargas' photography was mounted in 2000 by the McNay Museum in San Antonio, Texas. Her work was featured in "Hospice: A Photographic Inquiry" for the Corcoran gallery and "Chicano Art: Resistance and Affirmation (CARA)." Photographs by Vargas hang in the Smithsonian American Art Museum, the Museum of Fine Arts in Houston, and the Southwestern Bell Collection. She was the director of the visual arts program at the Guadalupe Cultural Arts Center for many years. She currently is the Chair of the Art and Music Department at the University of the Incarnate Word in San Antonio, Texas, her hometown. Vargas is a long-time admirer of Cecile Pineda's writing.

Colophon

One thousand five hundred copies of *Bardo99*, by Cecile Pineda, have been printed on 70 pound paper containing fifty percent recycled fiber. Text and titles were set in a contemporary version of Classic Bodoni. The font was originally designed by 18th century Italian punchcutter and typographer, Giambattista Bodoni, press director for the Duke of Parma.

This book was entirely designed and produced by Bryce Milligan, publisher, Wings Press.

Wings Press was founded in 1975 by J. Whitebird and Joseph F. Lomax as "an informal association of artists and cultural mythologists dedicated to the preservation of the literature of the nation of Texas." The publisher/editor since 1995, Bryce Milligan is honored to carry on and expand that mission to include the finest in American writing.

Other recent and forthcoming
literature from Wings Press

Way of Whiteness by Wendy Barker (2000)

Hook & Bloodline by Chip Dameron (2000)

Incognito: Journey of a Secret Jew by María Espinosa (Fall 2002)

Peace in the Corazón by Victoria García-Zapata (1999)

Street of the Seven Angels by John Howard Griffin (Spring 2003)

Cande, te estoy llamando by Celeste Guzmán (1999)

Winter Poems from Eagle Pond by Donald Hall (1999)

Initiations in the Abyss by Jim Harter (Fall 2002)

Strong Box Heart by Sheila Sánchez Hatch (2000)

Patterns of Illusion by James Hoggard (Fall 2002)

This Side of Skin by Deborah Paredez (Fall 2002)

Fishlight: A Dream of Childhood by Cecile Pineda (Fall 2001)

The Love Queen of the Amazon by Cecile Pineda (Fall 2001)

Bardo99 by Cecile Pineda (Fall 2002)

Face by Cecile Pineda (Spring 2003)

Smolt by Nicole Pollentier (1999)

Garabato Poems by Virgil Suárez (1999)

Sonnets to Human Beings by Carmen Tafolla (1999)

Sonnets and Salsa by Carmen Tafolla (Fall 2001))

The Laughter of Doves by Frances Marie Treviño (Fall 2001)

Finding Peaches in the Desert by Pam Uschuk (2000)

One-Legged Dancer by Pam Uschuk (Fall 2002)

Vida by Alma Luz Villanueva (Spring 2002)